The Nut House

Patrick Barb

Undertaker Books

Illustrations: JC Amberlyn
Cover Art: Dakota Marquardt

Collected – First edition 2025

Contents

Praise for The Nut House

"Imagine if you took the very best writers of animated animal films, fed them only a steady diet of the best cosmic horror and crime fiction out there, and then told them to write an original piece—what you'd wind up with is something like Patrick Barb's *The Nut House*. Startlingly original and completely engrossing (and gonzo), once I started reading, I absolutely did not want to stop, and I'm more than a little sure readers won't, either. *The Nut House* is probably the best (and most surprising) addition to the pantheon of cosmic horror that I've read about in a long time."

— Paul Michael Anderson, author of *STANDALONE* and *YOU CAN'T SAVE WHAT ISN'T THERE*

"After my initial *wait-this-is-about-f*cking SQUIRRELS??* reaction, my eyes quickly righted themselves from rolling as Barb's skilled prose and gory brutality pinned me in place and kept me there, rooting for those furry babies to make it out of The Nut House alive. But of course with any great horror story, it's best not to get attached, and this was no exception. Gruesome, bloody, and original, *The Nut House* has officially made me a "squorror" convert."

— Chloe York, author of *OUR DEVIL'S AWAKE*

"THE NUT HOUSE is a thrilling, darkly whimsical ride into the furry world of Asher—a burnt, battered squirrel with the heart of a hero and the look of a black-and-white cookie. When a life-or-death treasure hunt pulls Asher into a twisted crew of anthropomorphic misfits, the stakes become as nutty as they are deadly. A hoarder's house, twisted friendships, and squirrel-on-squirrel betrayals—every turn kept me guessing, hoping Asher would break free from his tormentors. This fantastical horror tale is equal parts endearing and terrifying. I rooted for Asher till the very last nut."

— Pauline Chow, author of CHASING MOONFLOWERS

Praise for Patrick Barb

"Patrick Barb continues to write original, compelling, unsettling fiction."

— Richard Thomas, author of *SPONTANEOUS HUMAN COMBUSTION*

"Patrick Barb is a name that is currently lighting up the horror genre. [...] I can't wait to read whatever he writes next."

THE NUT HOUSE

— Gwendolyn Kiste, three-time Bram Stoker Award-winning author
of *THE RUST MAIDENS* and *RELUCTANT IMMORTALS*

Also by Patrick Barb

Gargantuana's Ghost

Turn

Helicopter Parenting in the Age of Drone Warfare

Pre-Approved for Haunting and Other Stories

The Children's Horror: Cursed Episodes for Doomed Adults

JK-LOL

And One Day We Will Die: Strange Stories Inspired by the Music of Neutral Milk Hotel (editor/publisher)

Night of the Witch-Hunter

To Brian Jacques, Redwall *is definitely the reason for all of this*

THE NUT HOUSE

Chapter 1

The Crew

Asher Black remembers the tree on fire, his family burning as the dry trunk explodes from the inside out. Once-brown strips of bark, turned white with age, then consumed by orange, red, and yellow tongues of flame, shrivel to sticky black, like tar. A greedy predator devours everything in its path. Feeding off the air itself.

He remembers himself—young, no longer a kit but not full-grown. This previous Asher bounces from branch to branch, ears twitching, trying to pick out the screams of his mother, father, and siblings, all trapped by the relentless inferno.

When he closes his eyes, he returns to thick smoke and bright flames, so bright it's like the glowing orb of the sun's crashed onto Earth. In memory, Asher runs, seeking the chittering, chattering, squealing voices of his kin. He wants to join them.

He runs toward a wall of jagged fire, his hindquarters tensed, tail twitching. He dives into the fire, unconcerned for his safety. Tiny lungs fill with smoke, and black eyes bulge from their sockets.

The black fur around his face peels back on one side. Whiskers sizzle to nubs, then to nothing. His fur's stripped bare. Nothing will grow on this half of his face ever again. One part remains black, like the shadows, like the impenetrable wall of smoke that drowns his loved ones before the fire finishes its job. The other half's a wounded pink. Raw. Like he's regressed to a helpless newborn, unable to open his eyes.

He remembers jumping, expecting to go deeper into the network of branches, expecting to find a family member. He intends to sink tiny claws and teeth into black-furred flesh, then pull them to safety. He plans to save them all. Going in and out of the fire, not stopping until all are rescued or he's dead or the tree's collapsed into cinders, soon scattered by the wind and blown across the manicured lawns of the Majestic Forest neighborhood.

But he's turned around. The smoke, the insistent tongues of flame, something leads him astray. If it's not one of those things, then it's everything, working together to thwart his efforts.

Asher jumps through the flames and the sky appears clear before him. Its blue's threaded with silvered filaments of smoke coming from the tree. His limbs pump wildly.

But he finds no purchase.

He falls, crashing to the singed earth below. He lands on the ground where nothing will grow once the old ash tree and the black squirrel family who called it home are gone. Even as the tree burns to oblivion, Asher's on the ground, the ragged, scorched end of his black tail twitching.

He doesn't remember the sleep that follows. Or the darkness taking him into its embrace...

But they come for him all the same.

Asher wishes he were asleep now. Slumber's preferable to getting held upside down by his incomplete tail courtesy of two of Oakley Grey's heavies.

The gray squirrel duo's all muscle and fatty proteins without a kernel of a brain between them. Each gives the remnants of Asher's tail a too-tight squeeze. When the black squirrel opens his mouth, his yellow teeth move up and down, side to side, in silent screams.

But he won't give the bushy-tailed assholes the satisfaction of an actual squeal.

The gray squirrels hold him over the open darkness of a drainpipe bolted to the side of a single-story convenience store. The pipe's white metal comes wrapped in vines on the outside and caked in a slimy fungal growth whose dim neon green illuminates the ragged, rusted edges where the metal twists inward along the pipe's interior.

"Please, fellas," Asher says, twisting his body to avoid the sharp edges at the rim of the pipe, "you'll ruin my beautiful face."

The two lugs, Birch and Maple by name and trees of birth, don't laugh. Whatever brainpower they've got between them's devoted to the pursuit of tree nut consumption and kicking whatever asses they're told to by their boss. And that's it.

At least their fox squirrel handler DW, watching from the other side of the gutters, click-clacks his tongue against his cheeks, giving Asher's self-deprecating wit *some* appreciation.

Before Asher can thank him, DW's front paws reach across and dig deep into the scruff of the black squirrel's chest. He pulls up hard but keeps his grip tighter still. Asher ends up stretched across the drainpipe's opening. Face to face with the lanky fox squirrel consigliere of the Grey Gang, Asher shuts his mouth.

On his own for so long, Asher's talked his fair share of trash, letting those who might want a piece of him know to keep their distance. On the other paw, he's also grown damned good at knowing when it's in his best interest to keep quiet.

"We got witnesses who put you by the park benches near the water fountains."

Asher stays quiet.

"They put you at the spot of one of Mr. Grey's...one of *our* acorn caches."

So there's a cache of acorns there? Well, now, I'm not so sure I'd go around giving that information out all willy-nilly...to so-called "notorious acorn thieves."

Again, Asher stays quiet.

"Our witness says they watched you dig up and steal our..."

"Bullshit!"

Asher *knows* when to keep his mouth shut.

But he doesn't always *do* it.

Caught off guard, DW relaxes his grip on Asher's fur by the slightest degree. But it's enough. The black squirrel kicks off, pushing his hindquarters paws-first into the chests of the gray squirrel enforcers, slapping them with the remnants of his tail on his way to freedom.

His front claws slash across DW's chest. *Let's see how he likes it.* When he lands, Asher bounces off the gutter and makes hard contact with the black-tarred surface of the roof.

It's a short-lived, hollow victory.

Maple and Birch pounce, pressing their full weight on Asher and holding him fast against the roof's lumpy darkness. If it wasn't for the pink scar tissue on his face, the roof would make for the ultimate camouflage for the black squirrel.

"What's that again, Ashy?"

"I said it's 'Bullshit.' There ain't no way anyone caught me digging up those acorns."

He shrugs, trying to get Maple and Birch to loosen their grip. But it ain't happening.

DW grins, like one of the feral cats stalking the tall grasses between the older Majestic Forest houses. "So, you admit you *did* steal our nuts?"

"Buddy, someone stole your *nuts* a long damn time before I came arou—"

This time, when DW lashes out, his claws slice through the pink tissue on Asher's face.

This time, the black squirrel does scream.

DW wrenches back, keeping hold of Asher's skin. Struggling, Asher moves his head from side to side, still trying to hold back from the extreme response his pain wants him to have. Asher wants to make sure the fox squirrel's claws don't dig too deep a gouge into the side of his face.

DW gives a slight tug, as though to say, *Ya done? Had enough?*

Asher responds with silence.

"Let me ask you again: do you admit to stealing the *acorns* we buried by the benches on behalf of Mr. Grey?"

Asher remembers the tree on fire, his family burning. He remembers jumping through the flames and finding blue skies and loneliness.

Remembering, he nods. "Yeah, I took 'em. Figured you all had enough to spare."

The bell on the convenience store door rings below, *ting-tong*. Someone's coming or going. Human musk wafts up to the squirrels. Cooked meats in plastic wrap. The rich, heady aroma of coffee. Dried bubble gum, shoved sticky into door jambs and solidified by the passing summers, providing a sickly-sweet note at the end.

A scratching from farther back on the rooftop brings all four squirrels to attention. Maple and Birch get off of Asher. But he doesn't run. Instead, he stands back to back with the others, tails twitching against tails. Ears twitch, noses twitch. Eyes move everywhere, searching for the source of the interruption.

Everyone's on high alert. Everyone's on edge.

But when the source reveals himself, Asher alone remains tense. The other three relax, letting out a hearty, "Hello, Mr. Grey."

Where his enforcers are thick and musclebound and the fox squirrel consigliere he adopted into the gray squirrel fold is lean and wiry, Oakley Grey is pleasant and plump. He doesn't so much skitter to the gutter, as he hops. He lands heavy on his back paws, tail sweeping debris behind him as he moves.

"Mr. Black! It's been so long."

Since the tree burned. The ash was one of the last remaining originals from the old days when Majestic Forest was an actual forest and not a half-truth told by Them as They took over more and more of the land.

After the tree burned and my family's bones lay as powder in the ruins, there was only the oak tree in the park. Oakley Grey's tree.

Asher mumbles his greeting even as thin trickles of blood run down his face from the spots where DW's claws got stuck moments before.

Oakley approaches with forelimbs stretched wide, heading for an awkward embrace. "I trust my associates relayed the information we received. About the crime you committed against my property?"

Asher opens his mouth, but the tiny red dots on DW's claws let the black squirrel know he's reached a point where it's in his best interest to shut the hell up. So, he nods his head in the affirmative instead.

"Good, good," the boss squirrel continues. His arms close around Asher's shoulders, pulling the black squirrel into his gravity. He presses his bushy maw to Asher's ear. "I'm here to talk about your penance."

"Penance?"

Oakley pulls back, his face close to Asher's. They're nose to nose. Oakley's smiling.

"Of course," he says, "I believe in second chances. How else can we grow? Or learn?"

"Get to the point."

Before DW lands a retaliatory blow, it's Oakley, all smiles still, who delivers a solid rib-cracking punch to the black squirrel's mid-section. Asher's left bent over and wheezing.

The smile never fades, as the boss squirrel continues. "I need you to take some of my crew on a job. *The* job. The biggest one. You do this and I'll forgive your trespasses against me. All ya gotta do is break into the Nut House."

This time, when Asher laughs, no one strikes him. They let him go until he's all laughed out. His belly aches after he's finished: a combination of laughter, previous injuries inflicted by the gray squirrel enforcers, and the fact that he hasn't had a chance to sample the acorns he *did* indeed steal from Oakley's cache.

When he's done, Oakley's still there, waiting, smiling, Asher's expression changes as he realizes the request's a serious one.

"Wait a minute. Are you for real?"

Oakley nods.

"You know one of my forebears...a grandfather, great-grandfather, hard to say which and it doesn't matter, he was on the run from some fox squirrels, my dear DW's old gang, carrying a mouthful of acorns and a couple more nuts tucked under his arms to boot. This old-timer carried the biggest score of acorns ever. Certainly, the biggest since They moved in and changed our forest into Their *Majestic Forest.*

"But imagine one squirrel carrying all those acorns, Mr. Black. One hit to his neck, one bad landing on his stomach, and my kin woulda choked and died on the spot.

"But luck was on his side. Always has been for my family. He made it up top to one of Their dwellings, while it was still being completed. Not a finished home then, but a skeleton of one. Like one of our trees, stripped of its bark.

"Anyway, you know the rest, right? Sure. Every squirrel does. Hell, every animal in the Forest does.

"The gray squirrel ran from where he'd hidden the acorns, meaning to come back later and collect. Except he waited too long. I don't blame him...that part of the neighborhood used to be fox squirrel territory, not the most civilized location. Not surprisingly, they're no longer with us here in the Forest. Good riddance, I say. Right, DW?"

Oakley's consigliere remains still. "Sure, boss."

"By the time he got back, They'd put meat on the skeleton, so to speak. The Human-Female who lived in the house all alone moved into Her dwelling. She settled in for the long haul. Kept up Her repairs and got regular visits from the ones who put down their death traps and spray poison clouds outside. As if They have any more rights to the outdoors than us.

"The Nut House was locked down tight.

"You probably catch wind of stories now and then, tales of mice, rats, other ground critters, getting inside. But they never come back out."

"But now?"

"Easy, Mr. Black. That busted tail of yours is swishing back and forth like you've got somewhere to be. But truth is, at this moment, where you need to be is where I tell you."

Asher doesn't drop his eyes. He keeps his head up, staring straight ahead at the boss squirrel of Majestic Forest. His tail's sweeping motions don't end either. He wants to make it clear to Oakley and the others: he's sticking around but on as close to his terms as he can get.

"But, you wanna know what's changed? Why I'm here talking to you about the Nut House and not allowing my associates to make both sides of your face match up…"

Oakley rubs his belly as he answers, making slow strokes around and around. "It's the storm. Last night's storm. Lightning hit one of the branches on a tree near the house, not one of our trees though, thank goodness. Branch split from the trunk, and as it came down—*ba-blam!*—it caught the corner of a window in the upper portion of the structure."

"Don't worry, Ashy, the lightning didn't set the tree on fire or noth-ing," DW adds, leaning in like he's ready to inflict more violence on the black squirrel. The two heavies chuckle along with him.

Asher and Oakley both wait for the trio to finish. Noticing his boss isn't joining in, DW leans back, glaring at Asher. If eyes were paws, this particular fox squirrel's peepers would be wrapped around the black squirrel's neck and squeezing tight, then tighter still.

Ready to get on with whatever fate's got in store for him, Asher fires off more questions at Oakley, keeping focused on the one who controls his fate. "So, the window upstairs's the way in? What's to say the Human-Female won't have it repaired by the time we get there?"

"What, you can't go tonight?"

Asher rolls his eyes. He snorts hard, the breath expelled from his nostrils pushing down the fur on Oakley's face, like a blast of wind bending blades of grass. "You want the job done...or do you want me dead?"

Before Oakley or any of his gang can answer, Asher cuts them off with a wave of a paw.

He understands the answer's both.

Oakley nods, something close to respect in his expression. "No one's seen the Human-Female for a while. DW's been watching the house even before this most recent development. Right, Dubs?"

"Yeah, you're right, boss."

"The old Human-Female's gone. No stretched-out shadows against the curtains. Nothing moving for a while."

"Who's my crew?"

Oakley spreads his arms wide, showing off the other squirrels sur-rounding them. "You've already met most of 'em."

"That *can't* be everybody," Asher says, affecting a grumbling monot-one.

Now, Oakley laughs.

"Dubs'll fill you in on the details. Then, you've got one night to decide. Don't imagine you can run away though. We will catch you. Don't think you can hide. We will find you. And when we catch or find you, we'll tear the rest of the black fur off your pink, shriveled body. You'll wish you'd burned with the others."

Asher can't figure how the gray squirrel manages to laugh even while delivering his threats.

A Human-Child's first-floor bedroom window sits open, facing a well-manicured backyard. A wooden fence made from cedar surrounds a perfect square of evenly trimmed blades of grass. A metal screen covers the opening into the house, placed so the cool post-rain shower breeze blowing through Majestic Forest slips inside, but with links tiny enough to keep most bigger bugs and other pests out. Asher dives off the top of the fence, grunting from the injuries sustained at the paws of Oakley Grey's goons when he lands. He sprints through the grass, tail slashing against dandelions, sending white seeds above him like a fireworks display.

When he reaches the house, his claws sink into the sun-damaged peeling paint under the window.

One, two, three.

Then, he's up on the sill, scratching at the screen. One *scratch* echoes up and down the intertwined links. Peering through those diamond-shaped holes, Asher watches the Human-Child toss and turn in Her bed, dreaming under pink and purple sheets. Her black hair's like oil spilled over the pristine whiteness of the pillowcase.

On the interior windowsill, a shoebox's ragged cardboard top shifts. An undersized gray head pokes out from above a layer of white hand towel curled around the box's insides. It's not the scruffy, "dirt on your paws" gray sported by Oakley and his gang. This is the gray of storm clouds on a summer day, rolling across the sky in broad brushstrokes.

The creature's paws grip the edge of the box. Then, he drags himself over the top. When he's about to face plant, slamming the spruce-green pools of his eyes into the sill's white-painted surface, he extends his arms. The membranous flesh between his mid-section and the undersides of his arms is spread wide. He floats the short distance down for a safe landing.

"Asher, you scared me," the flying squirrel says, getting his bearings amid the glitter and princess stickers covering the spot where he's landed. *"So easy a caveman can do it..."*

Ignoring his friend's strange comment at the end, Asher replies, "To be fair, everything scares you, Flippy."

The flying squirrel, once named Willow but re-christened "Flippy" by the Human-Family who keeps him, folds his arms across his chest, hiding his gliding "wings" against his body. "I suppose you're right. *A little dab'll do ya.*"

The corners of Flippy's mouth turn up slightly, less of a smile and more the reaction to a memory of one he might've worn long ago.

Flippy and Asher go way back, almost as far as whatever unfettered grin the flying squirrel's recalling. There's a lot to read in glances and the slow, steady movement of a ragged black tail behind the larger squirrel's back. For squirrels, like any animal, the movements often mean more than the words.

"But you're not much better," Flippy adds. "*Do more, feel better, live longer.*"

Asher sighs, nodding. Used to his friend's fragmented way of speaking.

He met Flippy in the animal hospital after the tree burned. They stayed in cages side by side. Each fed from a clear plastic dropper with a black rubber plunger at the top. Sugar water—sweet and soothing. "To get your strength back," the Human-Female with big hair and bigger gold earrings dangling from her exposed brown earlobes told them, between her cooing attempts at a gibberish version of their language. By their cages, she set up a tiny handheld box with pictures, flashing lights, and voices emerging in staccato bursts. Asher ignored it, but Flippy grew entranced.

At least the feedings worked. More for Asher than Flippy. Asher'd lost everyone, everything. Without hope, he found solace in dreams of revenge. *But against what?* Considering their animal hospital days, Asher wonders if his single-minded motivation made it easier for Them to assume he was healed, to believe in his readiness for a return to the "natural" wonders of Majestic Forest.

Not so for Flippy. He had nothing to go back to, not even vengeance. The flying squirrel was abandoned by his kin, shoved out of their nest to the ground below. As he fell, he forgot how to fly. After all this time, he'd regained the ability to glide the distance from the shoebox to the sill. But nothing more.

A chance encounter with a Human-Family seeking an unconventional pet meant at least he wouldn't have to go for the final sleep at the hospital. He wouldn't have to enter the bright room at the end of the hallway where others went in...and never came out.

Not unlike the Nut House.

"You look terrible," Flippy says, eyeing the contusions and welts swelling under Asher's fur.

"Then again, you *always* look terrible. *Have you had your break today?*"

Asher gives his friend the single-clawed gesture and they both fall on their backs laughing.

"She gonna sleep?" Asher asks when they finish, cocking his head in the direction of the Human-Child whose snores join the chorus of crickets warming up behind the black squirrel, the insects hidden in their performance spaces between blades of grass.

"Yeah, she had the sniffles, so Margaret gave her some cold medicine...*M'm M'm good!*"

Asher shakes his head. He's amazed by how Domesticateds like Flippy absorb the strange words and customs of Them.

"I want to pick your brain about something."

"Is it about how not to get killed by Oakley Grey and his goon squad? *Maybe she's born with it, maybe it's Maybelline.*"

Asher stares through the mesh at Flippy's arched brow.

"Am I wrong? *Taste the rainbow...*"

"You're not...but there's more. It's part of it, but...I don't know."

With a sigh, Asher lets the story spill out. All the details about the Nut House, the job, and the crew he's saddled with for making the score.

Flippy listens, transfixed. Doesn't twitch at even the slightest sound nearby. Not the creaking floorboards in the hallway past the door. Not even the humming and bristling of horsefly wings flitting against the upper portion of the window screen.

"So other than the fox squirrel and Oakley's thugs, who else's in the crew? *What can Blue do for you?*"

"They tell me they hired Chee-Chee."

"Chee-Chee? The chipmunk? *No rules, just right.*"

"Yeah. She's gonna be there."

Flippy nods. "So, why're you here, Asher? *Like a good neighbor, State Farm is there.*"

"You don't know?" Asher asks, gesturing toward the inside.

Flippy's insights on Them have proved invaluable for his friend's survival in Majestic Forest. They've kept Asher one paw ahead of danger, avoiding the sudden death lurking around every corner for those animals living wild in Their spaces.

"Going into the Nut House...it's not like digging up one of Grey's caches in the park. Not like raiding a tree. I wanna understand how to navigate a house. You're my best bet for getting the kinda insight I need."

Flippy scratches his chin. With his other front paw, he reaches out and presses against the screen. It shifts slightly, revealing an opening to the outside world. Asher hops back. Surprised. He didn't know Flippy had a means of escape.

"*Fly the friendly skies,*" the tiny flying squirrel whispers. There's a sadness in his inflection, the meaning behind his borrowed words becoming a leaden weight on Asher's shoulders.

Then, with a shrug, Flippy continues. "Ask away," he says, "*You've got questions, we've got answers.*"

The next morning, waking with the leashed dogs brought outside by tired masters to piss and shit and snort up all the scents of Majestic Forest stirred up by its nighttime denizens, Asher meets with DW, Maple, and Birch at the edge of the Nut House front lawn. A curly-haired poodle, whose leash-holder's oblivious to Her surroundings, lunges at the foursome from the sidewalk.

All ringleted fur and sharp teeth.

A chipmunk with stained and crooked chompers leaps out of nowhere, imitating the barking of a much, much larger hound.

Ar-roof! Ar-roof!

Ki ki ki kiki ki!

The poodle spins around at the sudden appearance of the strange barking creature, twirling the leash in its owner's hand so it tightens around Her wrist. The Human-Female pulls back, yanking the dog onto its back paws, the collar tightening against its neck. Its panting tongue hangs out like it's dead.

Chee-Chee laughs, before joining the others.

"Asher," she says. "Other squirrels."

"Chee-Chee, nuts as always, huh?"

The chipmunk eyes Asher suspiciously. "Nuts? What's this, some kinda squirrel humor?"

DW clears his throat. Waits for the others to give him their attention.

"If we can please get down to business," he says.

Asher claps his front paws together and holds them under his chin. "Please, I'm all ears..."

DW's insulted, but trying to hide it. He waves for the others to follow as he moves closer to the house.

They scamper across the front yard, leaving behind the ivy-wrapped trellises on the front porch and heading to the back where the broken window's waiting. On the way, Maple elbows Birch. "You catch that?" he asks.

"Whatcha mean?"

"Thought somethin' was movin' behind the curtainwindow."

"Your nerves got ya hallucinatin', pal."

"Yeah, yeah, probably so."

They pull up short of the house's foundation. Above them, a long tree branch runs down from the second-story window and dangles against the creamy yellow siding.

DW holds up a paw. His gesture's meant to keep back Chee-Chee, who's got violence in her eyes, and Asher, who's trying to push his way to the front of the scrum.

Because someone's waiting for them outside the Nut House.

Flippy sits under the broken branch, enjoying the sun on his face, the breeze massaging his fur. He turns to Asher who's firing off a million questions at once but finishing none of them. "*The great outdoors,*" the flying squirrel says as though it's explanation enough.

"Who's this?" DW asks.

"Lunch," Chee-Chee answers with a snarl.

"No!" Asher says, "He's my...he's..."

His mind's racing. Normally, he's talking *himself* out of bad situations. Speaking for others isn't something he's had much practice with.

But he'll try.

"Flippy's the best home invasion specialist in the biz."

"'Zat right?" DW asks, not believing him.

Asher doubles down.

"It's true. I don't do this job without him."

DW spins around, getting up on tip-toes so he's towering over the black squirrel. "What's to stop us from tearing your wee friend to pieces? What's to stop us from letting Chee-Chee have her way with him?"

"*Alvin, Simon, Theodore. Doot doot da doota doot!*"

Chee-Chee backs off when Flippy starts singing jingles.

Like even she's not too sure what to make of him.

When DW turns to his heavies, they're not even paying attention to the Flippy-related drama. They're watching the Nut House. The black squirrel follows their sightlines up to the roof. A brick chimney rises like an angry thumb from the shingled rooftop. The way the gray squirrels squint, you'd assume the whisper-thin clouds drifting overhead were traces of smoke rising from the house.

But that wouldn't make sense, unless...

DW claps his paws together to get the gray squirrels' attention. "Hey, hey, hey, what're we paying you for?"

"Sorry, boss," they mutter.

DW sighs, trying to regain control of an already spiraling situation. "Alright, if this guy's the B&E expert you say he is...then let's have him go up first. Then, once he's up...you follow, Ashy."

"No..." Asher's protest gets cut off by Flippy hopping forward. The flying squirrel's front paws stretch to the jagged part of the branch, its lightning-severed and cauterized end still releasing a smoky odor.

"*First in flight*," Flippy says. "Don't worry, Asher."

Then, he pulls himself up the branch. One paw in front of the other. DW gestures for Maple and Birch to hold Asher back. There's no helping his friend here. He's going to have to watch.

Flippy scrambles, smooth claws scraping against bumps and cracks in the wood. He wobbles, the branch shaking the higher he goes.

The twigs protruding from the upper end of the branch, hanging off the windowsill like fingers, scrape across the black-painted feature. This time *everyone* on the ground notices a shadowed curtain moving.

Flippy's almost there.

"C'mon. Flip..." Asher mumbles.

And then, he's up. He's made it. Flippy turns around, gazing down at the distance he's traveled. "*You're gonna love the way you look. I guarantee it.*"

Asher shrugs the gray squirrels off. "Okay, let's go."

On the sill, Flippy's turned his back to the others and stares through the hole in the broken glass. He's the first of the gang to glimpse the Nut House interior. Something no animal's done in years.

Asher's halfway up the branch, the rest of the crew following behind.

Flippy turns to his friend. "Asher, you're not gonna believe it. There's..."

Stretching his paws the final distance to the windowsill, Asher misses when something grabs hold of Flippy's paw, yanking him through the glass shards on the windowsill and down into the Nut House.

Chapter 2

The Cache

Asher's black fur bristles when his front paws touch glass shattered to dewdrop-sized pieces along the outer ledge of the Nut House's second-story window. It's the same ledge where Flippy crouched moments before, talking about something Asher and the others in their ragtag heist crew "had to see."

Now Asher faces two pressing issues: finding where his flying squirrel friend went when he either fell (*or was pulled?*) off the ledge into the house and assessing the potential dangers *he* might face when following his friend inside.

He cups his forepaws around his mouth and calls through the jagged entrance in the busted window. "Flip? Flippy?"

"This is your B&E expert?" The sneer on DW's face is obvious without the black squirrel needing to turn around.

Knowing that ignoring the asshole serves as a more cutting blow than any quip he'd toss over his shoulder, Asher stays focused on the task at paw. His tail brushes some of the glass off the ledge, tossing the shards back at the others. As the glass droplets land like melting icicles crashing from the eaves of houses onto damp sidewalks below, DW, the grays, and Chee-Chee the chipmunk perform a group soft-shoe to avoid the debris.

Some of the slivers of glass remain in the black squirrel's coarse tail fur, however.

Good. Might come in handy later.

Leaning closer, poking his head through the crooked entrance, Asher repeats Flippy's name, whispering it into the unnatural darkness of the house. Something thick, a wall of darkness, *like smoke*, blocks Asher from picking out much of anything ahead or down below.

He's not sure how long he stays there contemplating the darkness and listening for his friend's response. However long, it's too long for the other lowlifes making up their misfit band.

Someone presses against him, too close for Asher's comfort. Figuring it's the fox squirrel, he's ready to retaliate in response to the unwelcome touch.

Except his glare's met by Chee-Chee, blinking her eyes fast, crouching. Giving her all in a *poor widdle woodland* creature performance. "Oh please don't hurt me. Please, please, please. Oh please."

Sensing the act isn't getting her desired response of discomfort and confusion, Chee-Chee rolls her eyes and nudges Asher aside. "Ah, you're no fun anymore, Asher Black."

He dips his head back from the glass, returning to the outside world. "When was I ever—"

But before his question's out, Chee-Chee pushes a paw through the opening. Asher falls silent. The tips of the chipmunk's claws touch the darkness. When she does, it becomes clear to her and Asher, what's blocking the illumination from outside is nothing more than the set of thick maroon-dyed curtains hanging across the top of the window frame. The thick, velvety cloth, like blood-soaked moss, displays rippled impressions across its surface, showcasing Flippy's downward path.

"Kinda hard to find your buddy with this here, huh?" Chee-Chee asks.

"Yeah, I—"

This time, Asher gets two words out before Chee-Chee's interrupting. And not with her teasing, unhinged sing-song nonsense either. Wiggling the nub of her tail, chattering in harsh tones, the chipmunk hops, skips, then jumps through the opening before Asher, DW, or the two gray squirrels can stop her.

"Goddamn crazy chipmunk."

DW's worked up enough courage to approach the busted window. Maple and Birch aren't far behind him.

"Told you there was something in the house," one of the grays says to the other.

DW, impatient with the current line of conversation, offers a firm rebuttal. "Knock it off, you two. There ain't nobody in there, 'cept for the lame 'flying' squirrel and the chipmunk bitch."

"You're all talk when *she* can't hear you," Asher says to the dark curtains.

Before DW fires off a "What'd you say to me, pal?," Chee-Chee's laughter rises from beyond the blood-colored curtains.

"That's what scared you? *That?*"

It unnerves Asher, the way the chipmunk's high-pitched laughter sounds so much like screaming. Closing his eyes to center himself, Asher finds the burning tree of memory waiting. With no sanctuary available, he opts to face reality head on. He opens his eyes, prepared to jump.

This time, DW *does* place a paw on the black squirrel's shoulder, pinching enough so it's clear what he's saying isn't up for discussion or debate. "Uh-uh, Ashy. Maple and Birch go next. Then, you. *Then*, me."

Asher says nothing in response to the news he's set as the meat in the goon squad's sandwich. He steps aside and extends his arm in a sweeping, theatrical gesture.

Maple and Birch aren't too eager to take the plunge. But when the lengthy nails on DW's back paws tap between the remaining glass shards, they hop to it. Their claws pierce the fabric of the curtain, before they turn themselves upside down, back paws pointing up and front paws to the floor. Once they're past the sill, Asher prepares for his leap of faith.

As he jumps, he turns for one last glance at the world outside. He's falling, but he swears he catches DW moving behind him, lifting the broken branch they'd climbed past the creamy yellow paint on the siding and onto the ledge. In this vision, the fox squirrel gives the branch a hard shove, eliminating the crew's expected way home.

Asher's too far gone in the darkness to witness that last part. But the sound the deadwood of the branch separating from the even deader wood of the windowsill makes is unmistakable.

Hearing the absence, it's what connects him to the trees, their leaves, their branches, and their seeds.

How am I so good at finding acorns? It's simple. They talk to me, they tell me where to find them.

The confession isn't something he's willing to share with others. Not even with Flippy.

When Asher touches down on the floor, it slides underneath him. He scrambles to find purchase. It's like stepping across wet leaves. The slick glossy magazine pages, coating the floor under the curtains, prove a tricky surface on which to gain traction. But Asher sinks his claws in deep, cutting through layers until he's steadied himself.

He leans to the side when DW tumbles after him, cursing all the way. Studying the curtain again, Asher picks out gouges in the fabric from one too many sets of claws scratching at it.

Turning from the window, Asher's eyes adjust to the dim lighting inside the Nut House. Going into the heist, he knew to expect the unexpected. But this strange scene's far beyond *unexpected*.

Flippy's on the floor, forepaws over his face, terrified of the thing casting a shadow across his body. Chee-Chee's beside him, laughing in a way that substitutes for the terrified screams the flying squirrel *would* make if capable of finding his voice.

In silent contemplation before both animals, a naked Human-Child, with black eyes like the squirrels', gazes down at the woodland creatures who've violated the sanctity of Their home. Unblinking. The child's head is a soft pink with cherry red lips pursed, arms and legs the same color. But the body's unshaded, a blank, nondescript white. More an absence of color than anything from the world of the living.

"Flip? You okay?" Asher asks.

Still holding his paws over his face, Flippy shakes his head back and forth.

Asher steps forward, putting on his bravest face to show his friend there's nothing to fear.

He stops in front of the strange Human-Child. Her eyes remain open, her lips bowed. Nothing's changing about her from one moment to the next. Asher stretches up, paw cracked and chapped, until a claw hooks onto the Human-Child's forehead. The hard plastic surface gives like the skin of an acorn splitting from attention. Asher pulls, claws scraping across the hard black orbs playing at eyes. Of course, they're not eyes. The Human-Child's not alive. Not a Human-Child either. It's a fake, an imposter, something made by Them to resemble Them.

DW moves in front of Asher again, using his tail to knock the facsimile Human-Child over. His claws tear through the imposter's stomach, extracting whirling wispy streamers of cotton stuffing. "Doesn't even bleed," he mutters.

Flippy scurries back from the false Human-Child's head. Lashes, long like claws, slide against those scratched glass orbs.

Rushing to Asher's side, he sinks his claws into his friend. But the black squirrel doesn't mind. He knows it's nothing more than a fear response. More than anything, he's happy his friend's okay enough to hurt him. He's pleased to see the flying squirrel moving again, no longer fear-stuck.

Flippy's mouth touches Asher's ear and he whispers, "*My Buddy, my Buddy, my Buddy and me...*"

"Hey Dubs, check this out," one of the gray squirrels calls out to their de facto leader for the heist. Asher notes the way the fox squirrel grimaces, reacting to the nickname their real boss—their real *gray squirrel* boss—uses. He also notes how DW comes on their command. Chee-Chee's stopped laughing, but she meets Asher's gaze. Grinning.

She might not be all there, but she's more aware than she lets on.

The whimpering at his side reminds Asher Chee-Chee's not the sole member of the crew with unconventional insights. Only Flippy's in no condition to provide his unique perspective in words indecipherable or otherwise. Asher brushes his front claws through Flippy's fur. He whispers, gentle, like how he remembers his mother used to when he was a kit. "C'mon, Flip, we gotta keep moving."

The layer of magazines under the window isn't an anomaly, but the beginning of an unfolding pattern. Past the naked doll—*yes, doll, that's the word. Flippy's Human-Child plays with them,* the stapled stacks of peeled-off tree skin sit, piled one on top of the other. They fan out wide from the bottom and narrow at the top, producing an informal staircase for the crew to climb. Placing one paw in front of the other, they scurry to the top. Everyone makes sure to keep their movements controlled and precise, so the magazine pages don't give way beneath them.

Asher's sure they'll get a better view of the floor's layout once they crest the top of the pile of yellow-bordered magazines with strange creatures pictured inside the front cover frames.

Except when they reach the top, they discover it's a mere hill compared to the mountains ahead. Glossy, unstable, stapled and stitched, magazine mountains. Some teetering on the edge of collapse, towering structures lurching to the ceiling. And not *just* magazines either—paper and plastic bags, bunched like wrinkled palms, hang between more solid objects.

It's a hundred lives compressed, compacted into a tiny space. The impossible landscape stretches across the not-so-open floor, reminding Asher of a magpie nest his father showed him once, made from stolen pieces.

One time and never again!

Memories of his father lead Asher back to the tree on fire, his father screaming for him to help and...

He shakes his head, pushing the memories away.

Pressed to Asher's side, Flippy whimpers another jumble-worded warning. "*Red Bull gives you wings.*"

"What the hell's his problem?" Maple asks, getting a chuckle from Birch. Before Asher says anything, it's DW whose claws slice across the chuckling squirrel's nose. Tears well up in Birch's eyes and when the fox squirrel hits him a second time, blood splashes in tiny dots across the magazines under their paws.

"You're welcome," DW says, but it's uncertain who the comment's meant for.

DW points from their lookout spot, gesturing at all the trash, the piles of books and magazines, the mounds of loose shopping bags and wa-ter-logged shipping boxes. Every creature assembled on the hill wrinkles their noses, confronted with a heady scent of urine and scat.

"Where the hell do we go from here?" DW asks.

Asher waits for the acorns to tell him where they'll be found. He closes his eyes. Ignoring the nauseating odors of defecation and decay, ignoring the crisp scent of sun-baked paper crinkling like autumn leaves, he reaches out in search of a tree. Or to at least the possibility of one.

Before DW and others question how Asher's meant to find acorns with his eyes closed, he opens them wide once again. There's one direc-tion he knows when checking for a tree—*up*.

Extending an arm, the claws of his front paw unfurled, Asher squints as he nails down the target for the others.

Across the space, hanging above the highest stack of detritus, a white string with a pearl sphere dangles, leading to an indentation in the ceil-ing. The rough outline of a rectangular door's visible once they know what to check for.

"They're in there," Asher says, letting confidence in his abilities and instincts carry the day.

"Grand," DW says. "How the fuck're we supposed to get up there?"

Asher tests the stability on the other side of the junk heap they've set as their temporary base. One paw in front of the other, he brings Flippy along with him. "We climb down and then up. It's what we do."

Climbing's not the only skill required to reach the Nut House's attic and recover the building's alleged treasure trove of acorns. Asher chastises himself for believing it'd be that easy.

Moving down the yellow-bordered hilltop, leaving behind the collection of slick, stapled pages, Asher leads the crew into a valley waiting for them between the garbage mountains. Here, there's another thin layer of abandoned life, serving as padding above the floor, but nothing requiring any climbing. As they pick their way across frozen smiling faces and old Styrofoam packaging, they catch glimpses of rotting carpet, infested with mold in spots or pulled loose into wild strands in others, like an expansive rabid beast hides beneath the waste, waiting for an opportunity to rise and sink its teeth into one or more members of the crew.

Asher's in the lead, but DW's not far behind. The fox squirrel stays on him like a mid-day shadow. However, Asher's got more pressing matters on his mind: finding the acorns and keeping Flippy safe. His forepaw slides through the top bun of an abandoned hamburger. What he expects to be rock solid proves a slimy illusion. The mirage of the burger crumbles on contact and Asher's paw sinks through sodden layers. Pushing, until he touches the carpet below.

With quickness, he withdraws his paw and uses his other forelimb to hold the others back.

"Flooded," DW says, stating the obvious so he sounds like he's got some control over the situation.

Asher moves along the border, testing stability. Maple, Birch, and Chee-Chee join him, pressing their paws against the edge and finding too much give every time. Asher reaches one side of the hall and spies a gurgling, overflowing toilet, with dark water spilling across tile and flowing out into the garbage landscape. Like the stone fountain in the park, but tainted.

He calls for the others, pointing out the best way forward based on his assessment. He delivers the news in as clipped and concise a fashion as he can, aiming to avoid arguments.

"We've gotta go through the water," he says. Pointing to the tallest peak of piled-up trash still standing ahead of them, Asher means to prove the leak stops short of the mound.

"It's gotta be dry there. Otherwise, it'd crumble right in front of us."

He's surprised when no one argues or pushes back against his plan.

Asher takes Flippy on his back, letting his friend dig claws into his shoulders for the journey. The tiny flying squirrel's heart thuds through his chest and sends vibrations up and down Asher's spine. Chee-Chee rides on DW and the two gray squirrels bring up the rear.

The water here's no summer shower puddle. There's no heat radiating up from a concrete sidewalk. It's cold and thick with a viscous quality to the liquid. Strands of tissue cling to wet fur. Flippy's extra weight presses Asher into the soupy mix. The black squirrel keeps his mouth closed. Even still, the foul pollution touching his lips makes him nauseous. His nostrils stay above the wastewater, sucking in barely breathable air wafting off the surface.

"Swim faster, swim faster!" Chee-Chee's got one of her forepaws dug deep through the fur on the back of DW's neck. She waves her other front paw wildly.

When Flippy whispers, "*Where there is man, there is Marlboro,*" Asher checks behind him and finds they've completed their slog across the muck pond. He lowers his shoulders giving his friend a chance to disembark. DW and Chee-Chee reach dry land next. The fox squirrel brushes the chipmunk off and she nips at his tail. When he spins around, brow furrowed, she's waiting. Licking her lips.

DW lowers his head and shakes himself dry with unchecked abandon. His tolerance heading toward an all-time low. But Asher's focus falls on the gray squirrel duo still mid-way through the muck. The blood from Birch's busted nose appears as thin streams of pale red, streaked across the mottled surface of the *liquid*. He's swimming in circles, blood trails forming spirals. At the rate he's moving, Birch is working himself into a frenzy. Finally, he stops and cries for help.

It's the other gray, Maple, who requires the requested aid. From the distance Asher and the others are at, it's hard to pick out the second gray squirrel. His head alone appears above the waterline. But the echo of his teeth chattering, bouncing against the vast canyons of refuse surrounding them, is unmistakable.

"He's stuck!" Birch calls to the others.

"What do you mean?" DW fires back.

"Something's got him! Come on, Maple, give it one more try."

Asher studies the face of the trapped gray squirrel. In doing so, he blinks. Once. There's the tree on fire, a majestic eruption of flames in the night sky. He blinks again. He's falling after leaping through the disorienting clouds of noxious smoke, his body breaking on impact, and his eyelids closing, but not fast enough. Not fast enough to stop him from noting all the gray squirrels watching from the edge of the green space.

Watching, *just* watching.

Now when Asher watches, he observes Maple's eyes widening and his mouth opening to scream in pain before polluted sluice rushes into his mouth. He chokes, vomits, and then chokes again.

Finally, his head goes under. Birch dives and comes back with his friend's face between his forepaws. But it's clear panic's worn both squirrels out and the rescue effort's coming up short unless someone else intervenes.

Asher flinches at the touch of a paw on his face.

The paw belongs to Flippy. "Go help him," his friend says. *"Just do it."*

There's new life in the tiny squirrel's eyes. His friend's fierce altruism moves Asher like he's caught an infection or had some curse placed on him. An obligation's strapped like a heavy stone to his limbs.

Before he can resist, Asher returns to the muck and makes his rendezvous with the gray squirrels. Now, *his* heart's thumping inside *his* chest, keeping him warm in the frigid temperatures. "What's wrong?" he asks Birch, helping him hold Maple above the lapping water.

Maple manages to speak first. "T-t-t-tail!"

Birch finds his words as well. "Har-hard to get a clear look down there. Bu-but th-think there's a tra-trap."

Asher bristles at the word. Traps are more of a threat for indoor rodents to worry about. They pose a problem for mice and rats most frequently. Squirrels encounter the baited death traps every once in a while. During late evening break-ins at the convenience store or during trips into the custodial closet and bathrooms at the park. As a result, the encounters are much rarer for squirrels.

Asher knows enough about a little to grasp the seriousness of Maple's situation.

Besides, we're the ones inside now. Makes sense we're dealing with inside problems.

It's as much introspection as Asher allows. He doesn't take another breath to consider the moral weight of his next decision. He gulps another big breath of semi-fresh, semi-corrupted air and dives.

His front paws and back paws work in tandem, slapping aside candy wrappers and dead flies, traveling through the sludge settled at the bottom of the flooded floor. He spots the wire-sprung trap, with its metal edge biting into Maple's tail. Not sharp enough to slice through fur and flesh, but enough to bruise, or break bones even.

More than enough to hold the gray squirrel fast.

Asher can't stay down any longer. He pushes up through the mire, hoping the direction he *thinks* is "up" proves accurate. When he breaches the surface, he finds less of Maple's head above water than before. "Can-can y-y-you...?"

Birch can't even finish his question.

And Asher can't nod his head or shake it *no*. He draws another breath and slips under again. His paws slash through sludge. He tries his best to avoid having his claws slice Birch or Maple's stomachs or pinch their limp limbs. But as his cheeks and eyes widen, as he feels the muck sucked into his nostrils and splashing against his exposed eyes, desperation becomes the color of the day for the black squirrel's rescue efforts.

His paws close around something heavy and flat. With strength sapped and air nearly depleted, he finds a silvered disc held in his forepaws.

Thick enough so if I wedge this piece between the trap and the gray's tail, I can...

A pounding headache sends Asher shooting back to the surface. Maple and Birch are both gone. Disorientation means it takes a moment before the black squirrel understands they've both gone under.

Asher clenches his forepaws into fists and there's a moment of relief when he discovers the heavy silver disc still in his grasp. Drenched black fur—sticky with waste—pulling him down once again, Asher takes another breath and dives.

So many things need to go right for what follows. He's got to swim to the trap through opaque wastewater. He's got to hold onto the disc. This means he has to rely on his back paws and the twitching remnants of his tail to propel him down.

When the trap appears in front of him, with Maple hanging loose and defeated above it, Asher works fast. He's dealt with plenty of acorn caches out there with dried leaves or burrs used to either alert squirrels to intruders or to mark guilty culprits. There's always a degree of precision required when pulling off a heist from those more security-focused stores.

But there's something to smashing through dirt and ripping out rocks, sticks, and clumps of overturned earth to get the job done.

It's this brute force Asher calls on now, pressing the disc between the metal clip and Maple's tail. Pushing up, up, up, until he feels like his limbs will explode. Until he feels like there's no more of himself to give and a moment of regret takes hold. Synapses fire. The burning tree's etched across his eyes.

Then, he hears whispering voices amplified beneath the water. *"You'll burn too. You'll burn too. You'll burn..."*

And then, Asher's momentum sends him rocketing to the surface. The trap's flung open. Before he travels too far, he reaches down, grabbing Maple by his scruff and holding tight. They breach the surface and Asher kicks for the comparative safety of the far shore. Over his shoulder, he catches sight of Chee-Chee and DW working in tandem to carry Birch back as well.

When the others reach dry land, Flippy brings over coffee-stained napkins, pressing them against the damp fur of the gray squirrels. Helping to rub them down. Both Maple and Birch vomit up the filth they've consumed. Maple's tail's bent to the side. He moves it gingerly, testing out its now-limited range of motion.

"Hurts," he says.

Asher's ragged, incomplete appendage twitches in sympathy.

"C'mon, let's go." DW takes the lead this time, heading up the tallest pile of debris.

The acorns promised are waiting at the top, through the door in the ceiling. Asher and Flippy bring up the rear this time. Continuing their explorations, Asher listens to the gray squirrels, consoling each other over their shared brush with death.

"Did you hear the voices down there too?" Maple asks Birch.

Birch nods.

Asher holds his tongue, trying to put the pieces together.

Progress comes slow on account of injury and exhaustion. But bit by bit, paw by paw, the crew ascends the waste pile like it's some crumbling remnant of a dead tree rotting from the inside out.

Caught in the drudgery of the climb, when Flippy speaks, the others all stop short. The flying squirrel leans close to Asher and asks, "*What would you do-oo-oooo for a Klondike Bar?*"

Asher waits for more. It's different this time because the others wait as well. Impatient, DW groans, following with "The fuck's that freak on about?"

Before Asher answers for his friend, Flippy finds his voice once again. "I always wondered how one gray squirrel got all those acorns into the house. I'm not sure one of them's capable of carrying so many…"

On his *them*, Flippy nods toward the gray squirrels.

DW laughs. Then, resumes climbing.

"Mr. Grey's relative was a resourceful individual. Not unlike Mr. Grey himself. When Majestic Forest wasn't even Majestic Forest yet, when *They* were new, building Their homes and destroying ours, he saw the writing on the bark. Back then, we had the grays, we had my fox squirrels, and we even had some black squirrels like ol' Ashy there.

"Except the previous Mr. Grey understood the trend of things with houses springing up every day and more and more of our trees cut down and the ground made so nothin' grew where they once stood. Grays and foxes fought tooth and claw and tail for the territory remainin'. Cuz territory meant resources and resources meant survival.

"The way Mr. Grey tells it, his relative got lost, turned around in a thunderstorm, found this cache of acorns..."

"And then? *Do the Dew.*"

Again, DW bristles at Flippy's interruption.

"Then, well he fashioned some system for carryin' 'em all. Figuring them as unclaimed. Never mind he'd crossed over into fox squirrel territory.

"He headed home and fox squirrels gave chase. So, this Mr. Grey made a mad dash for the nearest raised structure. Which I suppose happened to be this house right here. He lost the foxes and hid the acorns.

"Eventually, They demolished the remaining trees where the fox squirrels lived, and Mr. Grey let them all leave to find new homes outside of what'd become Majestic Forest. On one condition: they leave someone behind. That someone was me. End of story."

Except, when the story's told in those rushed, clipped sentences, Asher finds doubt creeping in.

Haven't I always wondered how the grays kept so much territory and every other group of squirrels got squeezed out? Hasn't it never made sense...the tree on fire? Wonder if DW feels the same about his story too?

He keeps those questions somewhere safe. To himself.

Within the silence following, the animals reach the top. Asher and the others find themselves crowded together, sharing space on the slick, rectangular cobweb-coated magazine cover featuring a Human-Female, dressed in white, smiling. Lips red and inviting. DW—stretching to reach the pearl globe attached to the string in the ceiling door—scratches the Human-Female's face off as he fights for stability with his back claws.

In reaching for the pearl, he tilts forward. Asher and Chee-Chee grab and pull him back. If not for their intervention, it's a near certainty he would've tumbled off into the myriad dangers waiting in the junk below. Once more, DW shoves them off and Asher's grateful for his years spent learning to balance with a damaged tail.

If Maple got hit, he might not've stuck around to complain about it.

"You, flipping squirrel or whatever," DW says, crooking a paw around Flippy and pulling him from his spot next to Asher. "Why don't you make yourself useful and flap up there. Take a running leap and grab on to the shiny thingamajig, okay?"

Flippy hangs his head, not meeting DW's gaze. The fox squirrel hooks a claw under the smaller animal's chin and moves his head so they're eye to eye. There's no escaping. "C'mon. Tell me, what's your name?"

Thrown by the question, Flippy answers. "Flippy. *Mikey likes it.*"

"Flippy? Mikey? Ain't no squirrel I know going by a name like *that.* Right, fellas?"

The gray squirrels, no doubt shook from their twin brushes with death, take a moment before nodding in agreement. DW presses on.

"Take me, for example. They call me DW, but it's short for Dogwood. On account of it's what kinda tree I got myself born in. You can guess what tree your friend was born in and Maple and Birch over there too. No big mystery, right? So, unless your Mama squeezed you out in a Flip tree, I'm betting you got yourself another name. A *real* name."

Flippy nods.

DW tilts his head as if to say *I'm waiting.*

"Wi-wi-willow."

Asher tenses. Ready to pounce. But then he feels someone's claws pushing into his forelimb. A slow headshake from Chee-Chee follows.

"Willow, huh? Like one of them droopy, mopey trees, huh? All sad like, right?"

Flippy's non-response is answer enough for DW.

"Yeah, that's the one. The one where the branches all hang like this."

Moving too fast, the fox squirrel grabs Flippy by his back legs and flips the flying squirrel over. He dangles the tinier, underdeveloped creature off the edge of the mountain they've scaled. Flippy squirms, forepaws battling invisible foes in the open air.

"They're like this, right? Right? Right?" DW's frothing at the mouth. Yelling his questions down at Flippy.

Asher pulls against Chee-Chee's grasp, trying to break free and save his friend. But she squeezes all the harder for his resistance. Drawing blood. She leans in close and whispers, "You move now, he'll drop the little one and it's the end of his story. Find another way."

"I'm sorry," Flippy says. "I don't remember how to fly or glide or anything."

"Bullshit! Bullshit! Bullshit!" DW's become a nightmarish motivational speaker, though what he's encouraging isn't clear. "You didn't forget how to fly. You're afraid to fly. You're scared of the truth. Right? Right?"

"Dammit, Dogwood, leave him alone." Asher's seething, enraged by what's happening and upset by the truth in Chee-Chee's warning.

His protests make DW shake the trembling Flippy harder and harder, until the flying squirrel manages to squeak out an answer. "Yes," he says, "I'm afraid. Afraid to fly. *First in flight. Come fly the friendly skies.*"

"Well, now's as good a time as any to conquer your fear, *Willow*. Time to embrace who you are. I'm gonna let you go in three, two—"

"Wait!"

Asher's call makes every head turn in his direction. "We'll do it another way. We'll balance, one on top of the other. Grays at the base. You and me. Then Flippy, then Chee-Chee."

DW's head tilts, as he considers the plan as presented. "Mmmmm. I dunno. Seems complicated. Maybe I let your pal go n—"

Sometime in there, Chee-Chee's released her grasp on Asher's forelimb, so he drops, his belly pressed against the shredded magazine cover. Eyes wide against his black fur on one side of his face and the pink flesh on the other. He waves his paws, showing his submission to the other's dominance. "Please, I'm begging you. Please, let's try this other way."

DW doesn't laugh. He doesn't smile or gloat. He reacts like someone who expected no less. He pulls Flippy back onto the garbage mountain and gestures for the two grays to get into place. They follow his lead, moving in silence, planting their back paws.

When Asher scrambles up Maple's back and DW up Birch's, they come face-to-face. The fox squirrel sneers. Then under his breath, he whispers, "With a face like yours, you probably always beg, Ashy."

Before Asher retorts, Flippy and Chee-Chee follow, coming to complete the makeshift furry pyramid. Asher holds his tongue. When Flippy crawls onto his shoulders, he asks, "You okay, Flip? We'll take a break. We don't have to do this now..."

But Flippy shakes his head. "*Built Ford tough,*" he says. Then, before Chee-Chee climbs on *his* shoulders and grabs for the dangling pearl sphere, he adds, "I wanna be on top."

"I sure love a squirrel who knows what he wants," Chee-Chee says with a throaty chuckle followed by her more typical high-pitched chipmunk chittering.

"Flip, you don't have to..."

Again, Asher's protests receive a definitive silence in return.

The tower of animals complete, Flippy's back paws digging into the place where Chee-Chee's black and white-striped head meets the more common amber coloring on her shoulders, they all work together, aiming for a one-in-a-million trick.

All Asher has is hope, since he's not a praying type of squirrel. He *hopes* the grays at the bottom hold their own, supporting so much weight. He *hopes* the bastard DW and Chee-Chee, wildcard as ever, do their parts. He *hopes* his efforts are enough and he *hopes* Flippy finds the strength to pull hard enough to open the door above them.

C'mon Flip, all ya gotta do is get the panel open when ya pull on the string.

"Almost got it..."

Just grab for it, pal. Reach up, reach up, and...

"Got it. I got it! I..."

Now pull!

Realizing they can all help, Asher calls to the grays. "Maple, Birch! Step back. We'll hold onto you two. Chee-Chee, you hold onto me and Dogwood. One-two-three. Pull!"

The old door creaks open. A little. Then, a little more. With a loud pop of stale air—*Whoomp!*—released, it's opening all the way. Chee-Chee leaps up and joins Flippy on the dangling cord, crawling up and then over onto the interior side of the hatch panel. From his temporary perch on the grays, Asher jumps, stretching his forelimbs, biting the air. Until he's digging one paw into the plywood and reaching for Flippy with the other. He pulls his friend close, howling with relieved laughter. "You sunuvabitch! You did it, Flip! You *really* did it!"

Asher drags them both up into the shadowed confines of the attic. With the panel dangling, it's easy enough for DW and the grays to scramble after them. Flippy lies on his back, arms spread wide revealing his membranous pseudo-wings. He sucks in deep breaths of stale air. Asher, black fur against black shadows, rests his forelimbs on his haunches.

He searches for light. The bulb above their heads is long burnt out. And whatever sunlight they'd get from a tiny oval-shaped dormer window across the attic is diminished by more tight-packed piles of old picture albums, video cassettes, dress boxes, and more. A lifetime of memories for the Human-Female reduced to mere obstruction for the invaders.

Wrinkling his nose, figuring sight's out of the question, Asher tries to sniff out the acorns.

He moves slow, deliberate. The others trail behind, but he makes sure Flippy's close. There's less of the rot inside the house here compared to what's settled across the second floor. But there's still a sense of abandonment, a forsaken-land quality for the Nut House in the middle of bright and sunny Majestic Forest. It doesn't add up. Puzzling out another mystery allowing his subconscious a chance to work on the more pressing concern, Asher can't help but wonder, *What happened to the old Human-Female? Did she leave like DW claims?*

"Help, I've fallen and I can't get up!" says Flippy.

Before Asher follows up on the cryptic musings of his friend, the black squirrel's nose presses against the squishy, soft embrace of something not unlike wild cotton or dandelion fuzz. He pulls back, the tiniest sliver of light shining through to show the pink and lumpy insulation, set up in the attic, covering the exterior walls of the building. Just as the darkness resembles Asher's fur, this raw pink insulation represents his own scarred, burned flesh.

He touches a paw to his ancient wound. Then, he touches the insulation. It gives way at his touch. When he pulls his paw back, a hunk of pink fuzz comes with it.

There's no more searching. Asher *knows*. The same way he always does.

"It's in here," he says. "Start digging."

Teeth, claws, paws; the squirrels and the chipmunk put their whole bodies into the work. Asher digs up the insulation with a single-minded purpose. Not so much to find the acorns, but to get rid of them. To let his debt be repaid in full to Oakley Grey. When he breaches the cache and the acorns cascade around him and the others, Asher won't even allow himself a moment to celebrate.

But Chee-Chee's gleeful, indecipherable chirps and DW's muttered "It's real. It's fuckin' real," serve as their victory celebration. Asher's seeking something to gather the nuts in, eyeing a lone sock made for a Human-Newborn, the article left alone in the attic without its mate in sight. It's something to work with, Asher decides. But when he grabs it, he notices the two grays.

Funny, how they're not celebratin'.

Of course, they'd worked apart from Asher, Flippy, Chee-Chee, and DW. When Asher moves closer, he picks up their whispering.

"Put 'em back, Maple."

One thing about the brutish heavies of the Grey Gang? They're not subtle. DW soon picks up on their conversation and heads over to the place in the wall where the two squirrels push the insulation back into place.

"What's going on?" he asks.

They don't answer.

The fox squirrel grabs chunks loosened by the grays' previous efforts. He pulls them away. One, two, three.

Creating a hole he peers into.

The choked cry DW emits while gazing into the pink-encircled abyss stops Asher cold.

When the fox squirrel pulls away, there's no chance Asher can resist peering inside as well.

Laid across the beams, he counts four skeletons. Elongated compared to what he remembers of the fleeting glimpses of his black squirrel brethren already consumed in the lower limbs of the burning ash tree. Black squirrels being close to grays except for coloration means the grays can't be counted as the source of the skeletons either. Which leaves...

"Four fox squirrels," DW says. When no one responds, he keeps talking.

"You know, I remember another story about the Nut House. Not the one they tell the gray squirrels like you and you..."

He slices his claws close to Maple and Birch. Driving them back against the insulation.

"They told it to us fox squirrels. All about the gray squirrel betrayal. Went in on a massive score of acorns, promised 'em they'd split Majestic Forest 50/50, but then turned on 'em. Killed 'em all. Except he couldn't take the nuts with him...so, he settled for the story, the legend."

Maple and Birch raise their paws. "Dubs, you got us wrong."

DW moves closer, nostrils flaring, fur standing straight up on his back. "My name's not *Dubs*."

Touching his scabbed-over nose, a memory bolt of lightning shooting through him, Birch takes the first step to meet the fox squirrel. Asher steps back. DW's foot slips on top of a lone acorn, rolled out from the assembled pile. It sails through a hole in the insulation, and they all turn to watch.

Pinging like hailstones against the cobbles of the park walkways, the nut bounces off the wooden beams and then hits a pocket of open space. Before it falls *down, down, down.*

Plink-plink-plink!

It's hard to tell for certain, but by the sounds coming up to them and the length of time they hear the acorn falling, Asher guesses the nut's gone past the second floor and slipped to the first floor. Where they haven't gone.

Where we don't need to go.

Flippy pulls Asher close, so their noses touch. He points to the hole in the insulation—with the dead fox squirrel skeletons and the falling acorn.

"The best part of waking up...is Folgers in your cup."

Chapter 3
The Coward

After delivering his cryptic sing-song words—*warning, prophecy, nonsense, who knows?*—Flippy's eyes roll back in his head. Pushing away from Asher's coal-colored face, he drops to the attic floor. The tiny flying squirrel's head presses into the insulation, so it appears he'll fall through, into the pink—a birth in reverse.

Behind the friends, the gray squirrels argue with DW in harsh whispers suggesting violence ready to break across the attic. Like a sky where someone's tuned the sunlight until it's too rich and saturated, warning of a raging thunderstorm to come. Asher's got no time for bickering between three squirrels who threatened him with massive bodily trauma less than a day before.

Instead, he focuses on helping Flippy. There's an ache at the bottom of his stomach, watching his friend thrash against the insulation. Domesticated, homebound with a Human-Family for years, the flying squirrel isn't fit for the dangers of the outside world. (And no matter the walls, floor, and ceiling surrounding them, there's no mistaking that the site of the infamous acorn cache is more "of the wilderness" than of the Humans.)

Asher reaches out and pulls Flippy to him. He holds his friend tight against his chest and mid-section. Nuzzling the top of his head, nipping his ears. Not violent, but reassuring. Making it clear he's there for Flippy. He's got him now and he won't let him go.

"We're gonna be okay, Flip. You hear me? We're gonna be okay."

"*Every kiss begins with K...*"

"There he is." Asher playfully cuffs his smaller companion on the cheek after he mumbles more of his non sequiturs.

He steps back, letting Flippy stand on his own and get his bearings.

"Ah-hem."

Black squirrel and flying squirrel turn in tandem at the sound of Chee-Chee the chipmunk clearing her throat. On the end of one of her tiny paws, the sock Asher found is now converted into a makeshift satchel stuffed to the brim with all the acorns found behind the insulation. While DW and the gray squirrels had it out over the urban legends on either side of their species divide regarding how the infamous cache got there and who's loyal to whom, the chipmunk kept herself quite busy.

She holds the satchel out for Asher to take. "You want?"

Asher's hesitant to accept the offering. But when he catches gangster Oakley Grey's trio of violence and criminality putting their tense exchange on pause and covering the distance across the attic floor, he can't resist lowering his head and letting Chee-Chee place the satchel around his neck, after she nibbles and rips a makeshift handle from the provided material.

Soon, DW's in all of their faces. "What the hell's going on here? Why the fuck're you giving...him those *nuts*, chipmunk?"

No longer standing behind their boss's consigliere, Maple and Birch push past DW. They tower over Chee-Chee and Flippy. And they've even got an inch or so on Asher. But he doesn't budge for them. Instead, he keeps his paws flat on the floor. Like it's another day navigating the gutters, drainpipes, and powerlines of their home, their prison—Majestic Forest.

Once the two thugs find their mere presence isn't enough of a disincentive, they shuffle back. Knowing where their strengths lie, they let DW continue to speak for them. But it's clear to any animal with two eyes, a nose, and a brain that something's changed in the dynamic between Oakley Grey's "esteemed" employees. DW stutters. Then, he clears his throat. Long and drawn out, like he's trying to summon his nerves up from the pit of his stomach. On one paw, Asher doesn't blame him.

Seeing your people dead. Then, waking up all these suspicions, and you're not even sure how they connect. Even with all the pieces available... I still remember the tree on fire. And the stink of something like Their gasoline and rotten eggs filling my nostrils. The gray squirrels watching...

But on the other paw: *Fuck 'em.*

"You expect us to let this *thief* carry the motherlode?"

Before Asher responds, Chee-Chee speaks up. Pointing to the grays, she asks DW, "You trust *them* now?" And then, to the grays, about DW: "And you gray boys trust this foxy squirrel?"

The Grey Gang trio won't meet each other's eyes. Chee-Chee, not giving a damn, keeps going. "And would any of you trust *me* with those nuts? Or the Domesticated? He'd break his pwetty little neck carrying those things, yeah?"

Still no answer from the Grey Gang.

Then finally, DW stomps his back paw against the wooden floor and turns, slapping his tail across the other's faces.

"Fine. Let's get outta here. Ashy, you and your no-flying runt stick close."

After the descent from the attic door and crawling down the trash peak, with Flippy riding on his back all the way, Asher opts to lead the others the very long way around the rat-trapped muck pile rather than risk another trip through it.

The crew navigates the longer way around in near silence. For a time, there's only the animals' breathing or the occasional wrinkle of old papers and discarded food wrappers under their paws. And nothing more.

Asher tries to focus on those immediate sounds, while ignoring the sense that the falling acorn's still pinging off ceiling beams behind them, under them, and all around them.

"You okay?"

It takes Asher a moment to process that Flippy's whispering in his ear. The flying squirrel's concern for his friend's well-being is clear. Before Asher answers, Flippy tosses in a "*Truth in Engineering*" for his friend to chuckle at.

"Yeah, Flip. We're almost done and then my debt's paid."

DW's snort of laughter hurts like claws slashed across the belly or teeth clamped down on a jugular. Asher stops moving, the sudden flare-up of mental anguish's so bad.

He doesn't need to say anything to Flippy or even exchange a glance with his friend; the teeny flying squirrel knows when it's time to get off Asher's back.

Asher turns to face the chuckling fox squirrel. "What's funny?" he asks.

Rather than answer, DW tries pressing forward, tries taking the lead back to the broken window. But Asher's fast, blocking his way. Stamping his back paws and arching a brow to make it clear there's no escaping the confrontation DW set into motion.

DW chuckles again and slows down. His drawn-out guffaws match his plodding steps. Asher dodges stray bits of debris as he moves backward, matching his pace to DW's.

"You believe Oakley Grey's gonna let you go?" DW asks him.

"We made a deal."

Even as the words come, Asher tastes their wrongness on his tongue, before they slip past his teeth and muzzle. Dread certainty itches at the back of his skull like fleas digging under his fur, burrowing through his bones.

"You wanna trust a gray squirrel deal? You wanna believe you'll live your life without being put in debt to the smiling bastard from this point forward?"

Chee-Chee's exaggerated *Ooooooooh* serves as the sole vocalized response from the witnesses. As he reaches a forepaw up and squeezes the satchel of acorns, Asher notes how Maple and Birch don't react to DW's accusations.

Something damning accompanies their acceptance of his words.

Seeing this recognition in Asher's eyes, DW goes for the kill. "You ever wonder what kinda deal *your* family made to keep their ash tree all to themselves? How'd *that* deal work for 'em?"

If he's going for the kill, he gets the desired result. Asher roars and leaps at the fox squirrel. Claws out on all four limbs, ready for blood. The momentum's enough to send DW onto his back, then rolling over again, so he's on top of Asher.

The black squirrel bites into DW's cheek, and he comes back with a mouthful of scratchy, salt-and-pepper fur between his teeth.

By this point, the fox squirrel's overcome his opponent's temporary advantage of surprise and sinks the claws of one of his forepaws into the pink scar tissue on Asher's face.

The resulting scream sends Flippy shivering behind Chee-Chee, hiding his head under his membranous "wings." Despite her gleeful reaction to watching more violence unfold, Chee-Chee still reaches a paw out to stroke the shivering flying squirrel on his head.

Hard to say whether it's a comforting gesture or not.

Asher glimpses the interaction from the corner of his eye, a kaleidoscope sliver of experience, as he rains down blows on DW's face and body, with the same blows returned in kind.

Blood trickles down the side of his face, before getting caught in the black of his fur. Scratching his opponent with deep gouging strokes from one forepaw, he holds his other limb against his own wound. The paw comes back thick and jammy with blood the color of the curtains—the last membrane between Majestic Forest and the Nut House.

Asher's got no idea how far they've got to go to reach the window and the branch—the one that may or may not be waiting for their escape.

One of the grays, Maple, Birch—*or it's both*, shout as Asher shoves himself free of their attempt to separate the combatants and barrels back full speed ahead into DW. There's a loud crack following the collision. Asher hopes it comes from the fox squirrel's body, but realizes soon enough it's from one of the trash piles shook loose by their violence.

As the pile's contents shift and spill, a domino effect's triggered. Thin drinking glasses, used by Them instead of dipping faces into puddles, kept wrapped in crumpled tissue, fall and shatter like razor-sharp sleet. The squirrels and Chee-Chee hold forepaws over their heads and run for cover. More cardboard, metal, plastic, paper, and glass, all fall from tumbling towers of waste.

There's no rhyme or reason to the makeup of the debris.

Everyone scrambles for safety, trying to get their bearings amid the ever-shifting landscape. Asher watches the gray squirrels gnaw through an empty shoebox after it falls on top of them. He wonders how Flippy's faring. But before he calls out for his friend, he spies DW creeping over the plastic-sheathed cover of some tome. Its interior plastic sleeve pages spill out in a halo around the book. Each sleeve's empty.

Asher flicks his tail from side to side, recalling the hunks of glass stuck there from the windowsill. With another scream, not giving a damn what he sounds like or who's listening, the black squirrel launches himself tail-first, ramming his body back against DW.

He slaps and slashes the fox squirrel's face. Dragging his glass-studded fur across his enemy's features. Over and over again, until DW's black eyes are encircled with rings of red and he's howling, begging for mercy.

But Asher doesn't notice the bleeding, moaning fox squirrel. In his own bloodshot eyes, all that appears is the afterimage of the tree on fire, his family's tree consumed by flames all those years before. Their screams and his quiet sobs those first few nights in the cages after the fire fill his head.

"Asher! Asher!"

Yes, Flippy called from between the bars, stretching his tiny paw through the thin opening. Holding it there until I lifted my head and let him know I was there. I was...present.

When Asher lifts his head this time, he finds his friend a few feet away, balanced on a precipice. Flippy's found the one bare spot on the entire second floor of the house. He teeters at the top of a staircase. The wooden floor's cleared all around Flippy and Chee-Chee, who's stuck by the flying squirrel. It's as though the duo's swept away all of the trash and filth found elsewhere, forming this oasis.

DW's bloodstained teeth sink into the looser flesh of Asher's limb and body, wrenching the skin from side to side, stretching and tearing the already damaged flesh. Not too concerned about this latest attack, the black squirrel smashes a free paw against his attacker's nose to dislodge him. His focus stays on Flippy.

"Asher! C'mon! We found stairs here and a door—the front door! We'll get out if we work together."

Asher moves toward the stairs, dragging DW with him in a headlock. The iron tang of blood on his lips makes Asher's teeth ache when he speaks. "Flip?"

It's strange seeing his pal with a smile on his face. After all the terror and violence they've endured, the simplest bit of joy's enough to make a heart ache. For Asher, the acorns around his neck, bouncing against his chest serve to drown out the bass drum beating of his heart.

Maple and Birch follow, shedding dust from their pelts. Asher closes in on the post and rail of the staircase. From this vantage point, he peers down at Flippy's discovery.

While the stairs themselves appear clean, aside from a faint blue layer of dust spread over the planes of each step, the first floor contains another coating of garbage. This time, the bulk of the mess consists of brown and tan packages with packing tape peeled back and torn from all their sides.

Like during the winter when Flippy's Human-Child tears open those brightly wrapped packages and squeals with delight. What got freed from all those boxes down there?

DW groans in Asher's arms. Asher releases his grip on his foe, letting the fox squirrel's chin smash against the floor.

Then, he flips over and spits up into Asher's eye. As the black squirrel wipes away the phlegm, blood, and spittle, more taunting follows. "You're never leaving here alive. They're whispering to me. They tell me..."

Asher moves fast, grabbing DW by his scruff and pulling him up onto his back paws. "What'd you say? Who'd you hear?"

He recalls his time under the slurry, rescuing Maple. He remembers the whispers pushing through the muck to reach his ears.

"Asher! Leave him! C'mon, we can do this! I know it!"

Bending his knees and stretching, Flippy's high-pitched voice echoes like a triumphant victory horn played on a battlefield emptying itself of the enemy.

"Flip, wait..."

But he doesn't.

The flying squirrel scooches back, his nubbin of a tail rubbing against a forsaken black plastic planter with gritty soil and no plant life within its concave interior. Then, he runs. Tiny paws slap against smooth wood. Like he's got his personal applause section, cheering on his efforts.

Until he gets to the edge...and jumps.

Flippy lays himself flat, extending his arms. His wings catch the breeze blowing across the garbage. It carries the muggy, heavy scent of decay, but also pushes Flippy forward.

Flippy flies.

Right before he passes Asher peering through the rails, Flippy turns to face his friend and whispers, "*Let's go places.*"

In this moment of peace, Asher wants to follow his friend into the promised land. He scurries to the top of the stairs, joining Chee-Chee in tracking Flippy's descent. DW and the grays follow, but at a distance.

Flippy makes it past the bottom step. He pushes his arms back, coming in for a landing. From the top of the stairs, it appears he's on a collision course with the door. Asher squeezes his paws tight, aiming to ward off anxiety. He'd hate for his friend to learn how to soar, only to crash again so soon.

He misses when the layer of boxes on the first floor shifts and shudders.

But he won't miss, he *can't* miss, the thick, white, bulbous head of the snake breaching the layer of waste. There's no time to avoid teeth shiny with saliva or the black hole of an open mouth.

The snake's winding form rises from a floor deprived of sunlight for days, months. Maybe even a year. It's larger than any garden snake wriggling through the parkland grass.

Something monstrous and exotic.

Flippy's left with nowhere to go. Nowhere but into the yawning abyss before him. Asher's grateful he's too far away to see his friend's face.

It's a good thing. It'd break me to see him. The awful notion pours salt in his wounds.

Asher makes out the gold-speckled eyes of the snake, gazing past the squirrels and the chipmunk watching from the stairs, peering through them as though they're nothing to the beast. Its jaws close around the flying squirrel. Those gold-flecked eyes glimmer like the flames on twin match heads.

Light from darkness.

Then, the serpent dives under the debris. Wriggling, rustling cardboard marking its disappearance.

Flippy's gone.

The snake's retreat is smooth, like it's swimming through pond water instead of solid waste. It's clear the serpent's had plenty of practice navigating the disaster that is the Nut House. His traversing of the filth doubles as an alarm. From every corner, the trash moves. Mini pockets of exploding debris mark the emergence of the denizens of this home.

With the first sacrifice consumed, the Nut House awakens.

First, the rats come. Twin bolts of starched fur and shit-blasted tails, wriggling pink, scratching their way up the parallel runners of the staircase. One, two, three, ten...more. A stream of ground-dwelling vermin with spittle flecks around their chewed-up and spit-out faces. They speak as one—talking in tongues, expressing themselves in riddles far more upsetting than Flippy's aphorisms.

Gnashing teeth, biting the air between them and the interlopers, the rat army drives the squirrels and Chee-Chee down the stairs. Any division between the crew's erased for the moment. Shock and fear take hold of them all, Asher, Chee-Chee, DW, Maple, and Birch.

Asher's eyes dart up, down, side to side, and all around. No time's left to consider what's happened to his friend. *Can't stop to mourn Flippy now.*

More creatures emerge from their hiding places amid the trash. The bugs come next. Cockroaches scuttling, moving in alien patterns. Flies dart and dip over the heads of Asher and company. Landing and vomiting, rubbing their black limbs together. Some rats milling behind the crew snap and swallow some of the insects, but others let tinier fruit flies crawl over their noses and across open pus-encrusted eyeballs.

"What the fuck, what the fuck…" DW's incomplete queries come in choked whispers. Asher jumps when the fox squirrel grasps one of his paws. DW squeezes tight, forcing Asher's attention back on him. His blood-heavy eyes suggest a separate nightmare all their own, going on inside DW's mind.

The unmistakable yowling of cats precedes the felines coming around the corner, called forth from somewhere deeper in the Nut House's first floor. Slinking atop the wasteland, the skin-and-bones-thin creatures, with their sunken eyes and angled cheekbones, shed fur with every step, then gather around the bottom of the staircase.

Rats above and cats below. And a menagerie of the other one-off creatures filling in the gaps. For once, Asher doesn't remember the tree on fire. He's found something worse, something more nightmarish and cruel.

The Nut House breathes the interlopers in. And then, it prepares to swallow.

Chapter 4

The Creep

The calico cat's fur falls in thick chunks from its body, as it traipses across the garbage-strewn foyer of the Nut House. Eyes wide and head tilting from side to side, it's clear the feline means to make a thorough examination of the squirrels and the chipmunk who've broken into *his* home. The dull burnished silver medallion hanging off his loose poly fiber collar shows his name stamped in blocky text: MR. MUFFINS.

Mr. Muffins likely can't read, and apparently doesn't count on the squirrels knowing what his tag says either. As a result, he's quick to make with his introduction.

"Well, who do we have here? My name's Mr. Muffins, and who might y'all be?"

Asher and the other squirrels stay silent. Between them, there's enough bad run-ins with feral cats to know they need to approach with caution. Those abandoned offspring of the housebound felines end up savage and uncivilized in the tall grasses between the more run-down homes of Majestic Forest—the homes whose outsides match the Nut House's insides. The feral cats strike without warning or mercy. As a result of these past encounters, a mutual wall of silence serves as their response to the scraggly cat's entreaty.

No doubt Chee-Chee's gone through a similar number of violent, life-threatening encounters with ferals, all of whom must now appear tame and sweet when compared to the bedraggled, unsettling appearance of Mr. Muffins. However, the chipmunk's response differs from her partners' silence. "Chee-Chee's the name," she says. Then she pisses on the garbage, letting it leak across the tanned box top on which she stands, before it rolls down to Mr. Muffins's forepaws.

Mr. Muffins wrinkles his nose. After stepping away from Chee-Chee's trickle, he licks himself. "We don't know you. So you...five...must've come from outside."

Chee-Chee steps forward, dragging her tail across the final dribbles of her piss trail. "Sure, we're from the trees. You all know trees, right? Trees?"

The hackles rise on Mr. Muffins's back. His spine's arched and his mouth spreads wide to reveal two mismatched, incomplete rows of rotted, yellow teeth. He hisses, his voice a reedy, shrill sound like an ambulance siren. "Outsiders! Outsiders! Outsiders! Come to steal from us! Steal! Steal! Who's gonna steal from us? Yeah, you are, aren't you? Yes, you are. Oh, yessss, you are..."

The switch from sugary sweet to outraged fury and back again is jarring. It even manages to halt the chipmunk's reckless approach. She scurries back to rejoin the squirrels.

The rats and cats join their leader's chorus, chanting, "Yessss, you are. Yessss, you are..." Over and over again. The clicks, whistles, and humming from the insects darting and dashing between the mammals indicate even they're an invested part of this mob scene.

Asher's paw rubs across the processed cotton covering the recovered acorn cache. The pointed bottoms of the nuts poke through the fabric and scratch against his paw pads. He moves to lift the satchel from his neck. "Fine. Here. Take 'em."

Mr. Muffins holds up a paw and mewls, his vocals sounding like he's straining to make himself heard over a thunderstorm. His followers fall silent. "Oh, what's this here? A teensy-weensy socky-wocky? No, no, no. You want to take our Provider. In Life and Death. You all want to take our Giver, our God. She Who Sits. She Who Reclines. She Who is Death!"

Again, the Nut House denizens take up the chant in a call-and-response fashion.

"She Who Sits...She Who Reclines...She Who is Death..."

"Domesticateds..." DW mutters. His crew stays silent.

Asher glances over his shoulder and faces the glimmer of tears in the eyes of the grays. Even Chee-Chee's restrained, her mouth shut tight. Waiting.

It falls to Asher to speak. "Now, sir, Mr....uh..."

"Muffins!" the Nut House animals answer as one.

"Mr. Muffins, sure. We don't want any trouble. We came here for something left behind by the squirrels like us. We believed this house to be empty. Clearly, it's not. We apologize for any disturbance we caused and we aren't trying to take away anything that doesn't belong to us. Especially not something, uh, precious or sacred to you all. All we want's a safe passage out of here and a return to the outside world."

Asher hates talking and he especially hates doing it for the animals responsible for his friend's death, but he hopes his words are enough.

They're not.

"Liar! Liar! Pants of fire!" Mr. Muffins screams. "There is no outside! Consult the prophecies of She Who Reclines, you blasphemers! The outside's an evil, hateful place! She welcomed us. Some of us she brought into the fold, others she welcomed when they stumbled on the house...this temple."

She Who Reclines...She Who Reclines...

Behind Asher, DW chuckles. Amused by his rival's failure to break through to the Domesticateds of the Nut House. "C'mon Maple, Birch, let's get the fuck outta here, fellas," he says to his fellow gangsters.

Mr. Muffins's phlegmy hiss gets picked up by his fellow corpse-thin cats. The droning buzz of the insects joins their chorus. When Maple and Birch turn to ascend the stairs to the second floor, one of the mangled, misshapen rats lined up along the railing lunges forward. Yellow teeth, like blades, descend. The rodent latches onto Birch's already-injured nose.

Caught off balance, the gray squirrel's back paws give way underneath him. He stumbles, but the rat remains steady with its claws dug into the hardwood on the steps. The arc of blood from Birch's face, pulsing from the spot where his nose sat moments before, covers the rat in a baptismal font. The creature opens its mouth, showing off the nose and hunk of flesh it's removed from the gray squirrel. Its cheeks fill with blood.

Then, it swallows.

Maple holds his bleeding, panicking friend up and they descend in a sloppy, unsteady fashion. More falling than any deliberate movements. Driving DW, Chee-Chee, and even Asher farther down the stairs as well. The rats follow them.

On the first floor, waiting on the cardboard boxes and envelopes left behind by the mistress of the house—*She Who Reclines*, Mr. Muffins and the others remain still. For now.

Asher's certain they'll move. He knows it the same way he remembers the tree on fire and understands that digging too deep for answers means facing the possibility of being torn apart from the inside out.

"My no-th! My no-th!" Birch's pathetic groans become thicker with each exclamation as blood trickles into his mouth and down his throat.

He's drowning, choking on himself.

"Bad, bad, bad. Naughty, naughty, naughty. We won't tolerate naughty beasts here. We're gonna take care of you. Oh yes, we are. Oh yes, we are."

Mr. Muffins's stiff tongue, the pink color gone a drab gray like spoiled fish, licks at his paws. When he glances up from his work, his tongue's covered in dust, fur, and dead skin.

Asher checks for an exit. He bobs his head, up, down, and side to side. He wishes the acorns would "talk" to him, offering any new, life-saving wisdom hidden in their shells.

But they're silent.

Hanging from his neck. Feeling heavier and heavier.

Something slides across the tattered end of his black stub—a rat's thin, warty tail. Already, they're closer than they were moments prior.

Too close.

Asher weighs his options. They're short one healthy gray squirrel, with Birch pressed up against Maple. And, of course, Maple's none too interested in abandoning his partner. That leaves Asher, DW, and…

…Chee-Chee.

The chipmunk's paw strikes at the rat's tail weaving between their legs. Once it's in her grasp, she dives for it, with her mouth open wide. She bites down with the same level of intensity she'd apply to grazing on one of Their food stashes left intact, unwrapped on a checkered blanket in the park.

The end of the rat's tail, detached from its owner, twists and twitches on the next-to-last step before the ground. The squirrels cling to the last step, resisting a final push to the floor by the ever-encroaching and now enraged rodents behind them. Asher assesses the bugs and cats, trying to figure a way past them. On closer examination, he spies tiny field mice, a couple of lizards, and a fat hamster, opening her toothless mouth in a slow yawn to reveal what Asher first mistakes for a wriggling pink tongue. But when the mucus-coated fetal creature opens its own eyes and screams, the black squirrel understands—with horror—what he's staring at is the hamster's offspring, hidden away in Mother Hamster's mouth.

And there's also the snake out there somewhere. Of course, the damn snake.

Every day since the tree burned and They returned him to the "wilds" of Majestic Forest, every moment of Asher's life has been a calculation. Weighing the odds, assessing situations, and taking measured risks. This way of living is a necessity because he is alone. All he has are his choices to keep him alive, keep him sane.

Flippy served as his sounding board, a considerate source of conversation meant to keep him removed from the insanity of loneliness. But Flippy wasn't a replacement for family.

And now he's gone too.

The injured rat retreats to the frantic caresses of his brethren. Their chittering shrieks are near indecipherable, but Asher picks out bits about "blood" and "vengeance." Lisping whispered promises to "the Rat King" sound between their screams. It's clear the rats pose the most immediate threat to Asher's survival.

The animals in the foyer shouldn't prove too much of a challenge if the crew works together. Going through the malnourished creatures appears to be their best bet for finding a way out of this bad situation. Not to the front door though; even the smaller, weaker animals are packed in tight, lowering the chances of the route providing a means for successful escape.

They'll need to venture farther back into the house. Asher's betting...hoping...there's another way out. Somewhere invisible from outside the Nut House: a broken window hidden by well-placed plastic blinds or an unblocked pipe wide enough to fit them all. Something.

But if they want to find the truth, they'll need to move. *Now.*

"Dogwood!"

Asher's shout wrenches the fox squirrel from whatever contemplations or calculations of his own he's engaged in, pulling him back to reality. Asher grabs Maple's paw. He nods to DW to likewise help the injured, incoherent Birch. Every instinct's screaming at the black squirrel to leave the mauled gray behind. One less body to worry about. Less blood for the others to sniff out and track.

But snippets of Flippy's cryptic speeches dig deep into Asher's brain. *"...the friendly skies... When you're here, your family..."*

"We've gotta run," Asher says, nodding in the opposite direction of Mr. Muffins and his minions.

"No! No! No!" the calico screams. "No running in this house, Fuzzy Wuzzykins."

As though punctuating their leader's words, a rat snaps its jaw close to Asher's face. Acting on instinct, he hefts the acorn satchel up, then smashes it down. Again and again. Striking the rat full force in the face.

Soon enough, the rodent's got one eye dangling from its socket, studying the grain texture on the step below.

Chee-Chee's laughter's so loud Asher pictures it as a solid thing.

Then, she mounts the rat, biting into the eye with her thick front teeth. The eyeball squishes like a bug, oozing its insides onto her fur. She turns to the squirrels and repeats Asher's earlier command. "Run!"

Wriggling tails and guts heavy with gas, the rats swarm the chipmunk. Teeth take hold of her ears, her cheeks, her limbs. As he charges forward, Asher won't look back the way they came. The four remaining squirrels work as a battering ram to penetrate the defenses of the few followers of "She Who Reclines" who block their path deeper into the Nut House.

But even over the raucous cries of the cultists, the damp tearing sounds and the drip-drip-drip afterward, marking Chee-Chee's destruction, are unmistakable to Asher's ears.

The linked chain of squirrels shifts from a horizontal line across the floor to a vertical, an arrow shot full-force but still flying on a crooked trajectory.

Hot breath on the back of his neck sends a chill down Asher's spine. "Move!" he screams.

The garbage crumbles behind him, the snake burrowing back under after missing out on seconds.

Behind them, the Nut House cult surges forward in pursuit of the interlopers. "The creep! The creep! Now, it's time to do the creep!"

Mr. Muffins's words precede orgasmic exclamations from the other cultists. "The outside world's a dead world. Not dead like our god. Not a death from which life is given and strengthened. A much worse death. Why else have they come? Why else would they try to take her from us? But she's ours to keep and so...and so...they'll do the creep."

Asher's got no clue what *the creep* is. But he's certain it's nothing good. There's an open door ahead, offering the overwhelming odors of spoiled meats and stale liquids left untouched too long. But also promising sanctuary.

As soon as they cross the threshold, Asher turns and the others follow his lead, slamming their bodies against the wood until it creaks, then clicks into place. *Closed*.

But there's no shutting out the chanting of the cultists, echoing the words of their prophet and leader.

The creep...the creep...the creep!

And there's Mr. Muffins still pontificating, elaborating on the specifics. "You creep and creep inside our house. We keep and keep you in our house. Sacrificed for She Who Reclines...on your flesh we soon will dine..."

Birch is dead.

Maple keeps him propped up on the counter by the sink basin. He holds Birch's head with both paws and talks *at* his friend's dead-eyed stare and parted lips that expend no more breaths. But Maple won't accept this truth laid bare before him.

Moments ago, Asher watched the life leaving Birch's eyes. Witnessed him taking his last breath, bloody snot bubbles popping in the wound where his nose once sat. The gray squirrel's lost nose was the kind young Human-Males and Human-Females playing in the park around the oak tree—the last original one in Majestic Forest—would *ooh* and *ahh* at. Saying things like "Watch him wrinkle and wiggle his nose." And their Human-Mothers or Human-Fathers might say, "I bet he's checking for some acorns or birdseed. Something to hide for the long winter..."

No one ever said those things about Asher. Black fur and burnt flesh, he was something they'd sooner kick away. Throw rocks at. Sic their dogs on. The sunlit park, the concrete sidewalks, the casual encounters with Them, all of it was reserved for the gray squirrels. It's how their leader Oakley amassed his fortune and powers.

The gray squirrels made Majestic Forest look good.

Asher's already experienced too much of the light. He's felt its stinging heat.

The darkness is more his realm.

But not this boxed-in, claustrophobic darkness inside the Nut House. Checking the perimeter of the kitchen once more, he tests the tiny window above the sink. It's still locked tight and no amount of knick-knacks tossed against the glass can break through the pane. Nothing a squirrel could throw at least.

Down on the tiled floor, DW crushes the occasional stray ant or pill-bug crawling under the kitchen door. He makes sure not to get too close to the gap between floor and door. From his spot on the countertop, Asher's seen cat claws swiping underneath in lazy half-hearted attempts to strike at any squirrel foolish enough to get too close.

At least, DW proves he's not *that* type of stupid. When there's a lull in the cultists testing the defenses, the fox squirrel calls up to the others. "Any luck finding a way outta here?"

When they make eye contact, Asher shakes his head. The baseboards appear secured with no immediate holes presenting themselves. He's sure DW's caught onto the same thing down on the floor. Even the refrigerator's pushed back into a corner with no room for any creature to crawl behind it.

He'd say something if he found a way out though. Right?

"Maple!" DW clucks his tongue hard against his teeth, getting the gray squirrel's attention.

"You're okay, bud. Gonna let you rest," Maple says, resting the dead—growing stiffer and glassier-eyed by the second—Birch on the marble countertop. The black surface flecked with streaks of silver reminds Asher of the night sky, viewed from the top of his family's old tree. So black and shiny, he wonders if his paw will sink through it too. Taking him away from here and into another world.

By the time DW ascends the kitchen island and leaps across to join the others on the countertop, Maple's standing at attention, waiting for marching orders. Whatever brewing beef appeared poised to explode between the fox squirrel and his boss's henchmen is put on the backburner. For the moment.

Fear makes for strange allies.

DW swipes his back paw along the raised burnished steel rim of the sink basin. He mumbles to himself, as though someone's right in his ear, whispering secrets.

"No...no...no..."

"Dubs, you okay?" Maple asks.

The fox squirrel shakes his head. Not so much in denial of Maple's query, but to clear the cobwebs out. Asher notes the faraway glaze in the fox squirrel's eyes. Like something's changed inside him during his time on the floor.

Maple moves to cover up his faux pas all the same. "Sorry, D. Dogwood."

DW's not paying attention to the gray squirrel. He's peering past the soiled dishes encircling the basin's interior. Mold grows over the remnants of sponges. If the squirrels hadn't already experienced the noxious odors wafting through the Nut House, the decayed remnants in the kitchen sink might have a deadlier impact on their senses.

As it stands, DW joins the other two squirrels in breathing out the side of his mouth, delivering his next words in a husky whisper. "There's a hole there," he says.

"What?" Maple asks.

DW repeats himself. He thrusts his forepaws down, gesturing past the plates, cups, and bowls, focusing their attention toward the exposed drain. Asher crawls over and peers into the basin as well. DW's assessment appears correct. With the drain protector removed, floating in the fetid waters of an abandoned cup of coffee, the drain hole itself is large.

Large enough for a squirrel or three to fit through.

Though who's to say what'd be waiting for us the deeper we'd go.

"Maple, stick your head in and check what's what."

"Excuse me?" Maple's already sliding down the streaked metal of the basin. Tail dipping into the dishwater, stale coffee, ketchup stains, and more. But he's staring up at DW, like he's trying to will another option to materialize.

The fox squirrel's not offering him one. "Stick your head in," he repeats, "Make sure we can fit through there. You're the biggest. So if you won't fit in there, forget it."

"Birch is bigger," the gray squirrel whispers, still in denial.

Asher winces, realizing this final trio he's found himself a part of consists of three lonesome souls existing in each other's orbits but never connecting. As it stands, DW ignores Maple's comment and urges him on. "Come on, Maple. They're coming..."

Asher listens. Strange how at this moment the cultists' efforts diminish. It takes a moment before he catches on that the stop-start roar he mistook for the heating of the Nut House comes from his panicked breathing instead. He closes his eyes, narrowing his world to the space behind his lids.

By the time he opens them again, Maple's upside down, body half in and half out of the drain. When he speaks his words rattle the dishes in the sink. "Dark this way, even darker than...but if I shimmy a bit and squeeze into...there we go..."

"What do you see?" DW asks. "Anything down there?"

Asher notices he's not actually keeping tabs on what's happening in the sink. Instead, the fox squirrel's head tilts toward the ceiling. His mouth moves between questions, as though he's trying to get his mind around the next words to come—words sourced from somewhere other than his own mind.

"I'm trying to make sure...we'll all fit...but there's some blockage here..."

Asher tenses on the edge of the sink, his attention divided between Maple in the drain and DW's trance-like state on the counter.

"I'm gonna reach my paw out and try to move..."

A skittering sound follows, and then a choir of screeches loud enough to make stale liquids spray from the abandoned dishes via the vibrations produced all follow. Asher acts fast, sliding down the basin's side to join the trapped gray squirrel.

DW remains on the counter. But there's no time for Asher to worry about him.

"Heh muh. Heh muh. Gabbbbgggggg." Maple's garbled words become further obscured, sounding as though his tongue's swollen, filling his mouth. His back legs and tail thrash and wriggle, showing his panicked efforts to free himself. It's unclear what's holding him in place inside the pipe. As Asher grasps the gray squirrel's tail and pulls backward, DW's chanting from the countertop. The noise carries to his fellow survivors.

"The creep...the creep..."

Buzzing, humming, then clicks and clacks, follow Maple's moans. Asher shouts up to DW, "Help me! Help us!"

When no response follows, he goes all in, wrenching back on Maple's crooked tail. The black squirrel plants his back paws until they scrape the steel interior, producing an unbearable sound.

It's soon surpassed by the tearing of flesh.

Asher falls back into a cup of noodles stained black during its long abandonment.

Maple's tail drops from the black squirrel's grasp. The gray squirrel's bloody hindquarters, still sticking up from the drain, split open and a cockroach hisses before it makes its exit. More insects emerge. Then, flies buzz through the ever-widening wound, covered in blood and feces, their wings dripping and shiny from intestinal juices.

A loud *POP* makes Asher cover his ears and his eyes go wide, facing yet another horror worse than he ever anticipated. Maple—or what remains of him—shoots out from the drain. The top of his body resembles a house dog's ruined plaything. Chewed up and spit out, with the Nut House insects splitting his seams. Their chitinous blackened forms become a second skin as they pulp Maple's insides to a sticky nothingness.

The bugs show no signs of contentment with gorging themselves on the ruin of Maple. They scurry forward, heading for Asher. He's too tired for any of it. There's no time for losing his mind...or his life. *Not today.* He slaps a pair of flies away as they try to burrow into his ears. His already ruined tail gets picked at by a roach's mandibles, his fur pulled out in chunks, but he keeps climbing, slashing his attackers with the bits of glass still stuck to him.

Up and over a stack of plates, past coffee cup shards, he climbs until he reaches the rim of the sink and holds a paw out, trying to get hold of something to steady himself with and pull up the final quarter inch.

A paw closes around his. There's DW, swatting bugs off the side of the sink with his free paws, and pulling Asher onto the countertop. The fox squirrel's paw pads are slick to the touch like he's drenched in sweat...but sticky like honey.

When Asher's out of the sink, he collapses in a heap on the counter. Panting, trying to catch his breath and crawl farther away from the torrent of pests spilling up from the sink. He ignores the choked sobs coming from his body. "Come on, I got you," DW tells him.

Once he's got Asher back on his paws, the fox squirrel touches the burnt side of his face. Patting him once, twice. They turn back to the sink. Asher struggles to get away because they're moving in the wrong direction. He's forced to face the shiny mirrored knobs on the sink. In his reflection, he finds DW's bloody paw prints, marking him. Behind him, Birch's corpse leaks rich serum from a jagged bite mark on his neck. The useless substances oozes forth slow and steady.

Like honey.

Then, there's DW with fur and flesh between his teeth, pointing up. Above the sink, a vent with loosened screws pops open and Mr. Muffins stares at the chaotic scene below. A pleased expression pushes his whiskers back against his face.

"They've whispered to me, too!" DW screams.

With the fox squirrel's maddening declaration, Mr. Muffins drops from his perch. When he lands, the cat slaps a meaty paw against the back of Asher's head. The black squirrel crumbles, returning to the darkness once again.

Chapter 5

The Corpse

Asher's alive, but he's got serious doubts now about what *being alive* even means.

Being alive in a nightmare? What's that, but living through the pains of death without the peace that comes at the end of dying?

When he opens his eyes, death surrounds him. From the garbage-infested wastelands hidden behind the otherwise nondescript, unmemorable exterior of the Nut House to the ruined corpses of the two gray squirrels Maple and Birch, and Chee-Chee the chipmunk, laid out on a teal-cushioned loveseat wrapped in plastic. The material reminds Asher of what they lay over dead animals found in the park or on the streets and sidewalks of Majestic Forest, before they're scooped up and thrown away like so much trash.

The brick hues of dried blood on the clear sheeting appear too plentiful for all the stains to have come from Asher's trio of accomplices.

When the snake slithers from the crowd, and the rats, cats, and the few other mammals part to clear the way, then Asher regains his senses and makes a move to run once again. Before he gets too far—or even moves at all, paws hold his limbs. His tail too. One set of paws belongs to DW, who's now become a true believer, embracing the worship of She Who Reclines.

Asher knows his rival's too far gone because he's left the fabled cache of acorns they recovered—their sole reason for venturing inside the Nut House—unremarked upon.

"Uh uh, Ashy," the fox squirrel whispers, "you've gotta watch. They told me about this part of their...*our* ceremonies. Told me about how She purchased Hiss Honor, the snake there, from the back of a catalog. Right before her passage through Death. Hiss Honor was meant to get rid of what She called 'pests'... But when she opened the box with the serpent inside, he kissed her hand. In the end, She Who Reclines returned to her throne, descending and ascending all at once. Now, she provides. No matter where *we* come from. I'm certain it's glorious. Watch..."

DW's forepaws grab Asher's face from behind his head, forcing the black squirrel's eyelids open and making sure there's no way he'll miss what follows.

The gagging, choking sounds from deep inside Hiss Honor—*a silly name, a Domesticated's name*—echo through the gathering place the others call the "Living Room." An ironically named location, finishing a close second to the concrete, brick, and asphalt world of *Majestic Forest*.

The snake's bile stench adds another note of rot to the insides of the Nut House. With one last rattling cough, he expels the partially-digested remnants of Asher's friend Flippy.

Another Domesticated with a—what do they call them?—pet's name. Like Hiss Honor or Mr. Muffins.

Could Flippy have ended up like these maniacs? If the wrong person took him home, would Flippy have become the one inflicting all of this suffering?

With adrenaline and rage pumping through his body beneath his black fur, Asher breaks free for a moment. He slices his claws across DW's face, digging them into the other squirrel's flesh and twisting as he's pulled away by the other Nut House acolytes. One of the skeletal cats slices her claws against the back of Asher's neck and he drops to all fours. Blood flows in a slow, but unavoidable, leak.

Asher knows he's lost a lot of blood in a very little period of time. He doesn't need the hot pain pressing down on him or the melted copper tang in his mouth to realize this truth.

"Enough!"

The command comes from somewhere deeper in the room.

The voice belongs to Mr. Muffins.

Again, the crowd parts to let the calico pass.

He doesn't stop in front of Asher and those holding the black squirrel tight. No, the cat keeps padding along. Traipsing past them with head held high, raised tail swishing from side to side. His belly heavy with blisters, sores, and tumors, he still moves like a shooting star.

Like, what was it Flippy's Human-Child called the flying squirrel in Her sentimental moments?

"Jesus's Perfectest Little Angel."

Asher tracks the calico's progress. Again, he doesn't have much choice in the matter, given the paws holding him, moving him like a puppet. At least this time, though he's loath to admit it, there's a strong undercurrent of curiosity coursing through him, making him a somewhat more willing participant.

As it turns out, the loveseat where the animals displayed the corpses of the trespassers was turned around from its usual placement. So, in truth, it serves as an additional gateway, another passage, taking those who cross its threshold deeper into the Nut House's most secret and sacred space. The animals make their sojourn beneath it. Mr. Muffins parts the plastic curtains to give his followers access to the Unholy Land.

On the other side, a wooden table, smooth and lifeless. Past that, the bricks of a hearth and the gaping black-and-gray-smeared mouth of a smoldering fireplace. A stack of paperback romance novels sits in the ashes, decorated with tiny flames burning slow and steady.

The black squirrel tenses. Someone squeezes him tighter and he knows it's DW.

Mr. Mittens parts the throng of worshippers and drags his bloat onto the hearth. "Who brings us here today?"

"She Who Sits..."

"Who loves us unconditionally, even though we cannot understand her words...or her silences?"

"She Who Reclines..."

"Who must we embrace, protect, feed upon, and sacrifice for?"

"She Who is Death."

Behind the calico cult leader, a pair of rats work in unison to twist a silver knob set in the wall beside the fireplace. There's a huff like a dying dog's last breath and a jet of flame squirts across the yellowed paper kindling. It catches quick and burns, illuminating the rest of the living room.

At first, when Asher notices the reclining chair tilted back ever so slightly, he's sure there's nothing more before him than a pile of clothing. A bundle of sweaters, full jumpers covered by cardigans buttoned to their neck holes. He's certain the long denim skirt hanging off the seat isn't filled with anything other than air.

Asher chooses to believe he's staring at another pile of nothing so much as nothing at all. More of the magpie-nest hodgepodge typical of the Nut House's overstuffed interior.

He keeps up this delusion until he's forced to look closer and deeper by those creatures controlling his limbs. Then, he's made to understand what's in the reclining chair, waiting to be worshipped.

First, he finds the green-gray face of an Elder Human-Female. *The Elder Human-Female of the Nut House.* Her mouth hangs open, no teeth visible. Cheeks sunken, wrinkled, and yellowed like the pages of old paperbacks left out in the rain. Where eyes should go, Asher instead encounters twin voids, the sockets cleaned out.

"Did you ever even see her leave?" Asher asks DW.

In return, he receives sharp, quick nips on his back from a few of the overzealous rats holding him. He bites his bottom lip to stop from screaming. Once more, he's found himself in another impossible situation where he refuses to show his captors and tormentors any reaction to their otherwise brutal treatment.

"Silence!"

Mr. Muffins delivers his command from the hearth. And everyone obeys. Including Asher. After all, he's run out of immediate options. Instead, he waits and watches. His eyes dart between the Elder Human-Corpse who sits still and eternal in her chair and the fireplace where burning books shrink in size, page by page, with each passing second.

"We gather in the room of the living as we've done for many days since She Who Reclines sat down and ascended to this higher form. In gathering, we make a sacrifice, choosing several of our flock to show our loyalty to the Death God—the caregiver and life-taker. We're all good boys and girls. Yes, we are."

Again, the worshippers answer, "Yes, we are!"

DW's breath, hot and rancid with blood and gray squirrel meat, worms its way around the curvature of Asher's inner ear. "Yes, we are!"

Mr. Muffins hops down from the hearth and pads over to the reclining chair. He rubs his backside against the stiff denim material of the Human-Corpse's dress. He catches it at the right angle where the denim rises from the floor. Asher peeks at feet once bloated and blistered, now popped open white, oozing yellows and reds down purpled toes and blackened toenails. Tiny bites line both sides of the exposed feet, the rough kisses of her worshippers.

Mr. Muffins purrs, long and loud. Then longer still. Asher wonders if the drawn-out nature of the ceremonies is common or something put on special for him—the outsider.

And DW too. He's trying to become one of them. But he's not.

Poor bastard never learns.

Mr. Muffins stands at the feet of the Nut House's Death God and addresses his flock. "A blessed day's arrived as we've received new blood into our sanctuary. Interlopers attempting to steal from us—to steal our sitting, reclining, forever dying god—have learned the consequences for those trespassers not of the faith."

The calico clambers up onto the lap of the dried-out, close-to-mummified corpse. When he presses his bottom against the folds in the clothing, dust, dead skin, and a sheen of sick all fly from the corpse's face. They produce an afterimage of the slack-jawed, empty-eyed visage hanging in the air for a moment. Separate from the reclining chair, the dead woman, and her favorite kitty-cat.

Then, Mr. Muffins turns and pulls at the round plastic buttons holding the cardigan in place. He hooks his claws through one eyehole and pops a button free from its secure location. He pulls the woolen material apart with his teeth. Then he undoes another, then another, all the way down until his work's done.

The wool cardigans hang loose and separated like a cracked-open rib cage. And that's exactly what waits beyond the layers of clothing over Her upper body. Past holes chewed straight through the cashmere and cotton, the old Human-Female's chest is split open, skin and bones hanging on either side like a cabinet that won't close. Asher's made to gaze into an abyss cleaned of blood, bones, and organs. The spinal cord, stiff and ramrod straight, holds the Death God's emptied skin sack in place.

Mr. Muffins scrambles to find purchase with his extended claws against the ragged edges of Her decayed flesh. Then, in a fluid, strange, yet beautiful motion, he slips inside. Claws scratch through dried flesh and cloth, as he stretches. Tiny indentations, showing the white hooks pressed against stiffened, yellow flesh and the rigid clothing layers, reveal themselves. Then, the calico sticks his head from the gaping cavity, returning to the worshippers from a stint in the abyss.

His eyes roll back white and a thin, shimmery layer of drool spills from the sides of his mouth. If it's an act, it's a damn good one as far as Asher's concerned. The cat's got himself believing it. Here in the Nut House, belief matters the most.

"Tonight, as the darkness reaches its peak, before the wicked sun puts forth its harmful rays on the cursed earth outside this home, we gather to render judgment. No..."

No?

"No, we gather to *receive* judgment and to ensure the proscribed punishments are meted out. She Who Reclines speaks through me. And

She tells me...oh my sweetykins, we'll make the trespassers burn. They'll burn, burn, burn."

Again, the animals take up the chant. "Burn. Burn. Burn."

Growling, hissing, spitting, and scratching at the floor, the additional noise provides the rhythmic accompaniment to the invocation. Asher closes his eyes.

I remember the tree on fire. I've never forgotten it. Sometimes at my lowest, I convince myself I never escaped the tree or the fire. It's taken me longer than most to burn, that's all. But I always knew I would.

The fire always knew too.

After the corrupted calico issues the ruling from inside the chest of the dead Human-Female, Asher's stunned and rocks forward at the sound of a sudden shriek.

He's shocked because his lips and tongue aren't the source of the scream. He turns, staring in wide-eyed astonishment, as a gang of cats and rats pull DW away.

"What're you...what's happening...?"

There's genuine panic and pain in DW's voice. The questions come like heavy sobs, demonstrating that he already knows the answers to come. His body's responding perfectly, even if his brain hasn't caught up to reality.

A smaller group of worshippers hold Asher in place, but the stronger members of the group step away to take control of DW. The fox squirrel twists, wrenching his thin body into strange configurations, yet finding no relief from his captors. They pull him across the floor while Mr. Muffins peers out from the open wound of the dead Human-Female.

"Please, you can't do this! I helped you! I want to worship! I want to worship like all of you!"

Mr. Muffins hisses at DW's protests. An eerie silence falls across the room, leaving only DW's whimpering and the crackle of a dying fire.

"But you're not like us," the calico says. "You came to take. 'They always come and take,' She Who Reclines used to tell us. Bills and mortgages and family members wanting money. More and more and more...we'd watch her take those pieces of paper and burn them. One after the other. And in Her honor, we burn our problems as well."

The animals who don't hold either Asher or DW clamber onto the hearth and blow hissing breaths at the smoldering embers. *They're making the fire grow*, Asher realizes. Again, rats team up to turn the silver knob. They hang from the bulbous protrusion, twisting it to one side until the smell of gas fills the room. Asher's eyes water and he wants to gag. But he holds in the stomach acid and blood he'd otherwise expel.

Not now.

Not yet...

The mob presses DW toward the smoldering flames and he moans, a forlorn wail containing years—generations even—of sadness and pain.

But as his paw pads and stomach drag across the fire, his wiry fur won't burst into flames. There's no doubt it hurts, but the cultists' faces make it clear: they never expected this rather anticlimactic result.

"Clear the way! Clear the way!"

Hiss Honor, the snake, weaves across the floor, in a stop-and-start fashion. He bumps against the coffee table. Asher discovers the clicking sound accompanying the snake's movements comes from the long barbecue lighter clamped between the serpent's unhinged jaws. The long spout sticks in his craw as though his tongue's blackened and hardened.

"Ah ah ah ah ah." The snake's words sound like a litany of Amens, as he nears the spot doubling as sacrificial altar.

The animals on the hearth form a chain, holding some of the smaller critters by their tails and lowering them from the edge, to reach down and take hold of the lighter. Then, they're pulled back up onto the bricks. All those tiny paws, tails, and pebble-sized teeth work together, teamwork the likes of which puts Asher's makeshift heist crew to shame.

Asher's got no time for fascination though. There's no free moment to wonder at the display of cooperation and ingenuity exhibited by the Nut House's denizens. He's too busy rolling his shoulders, testing the strength of those who still hold him in place, searching for their weak spots.

He tries not to seem too obvious about his efforts. Even with everyone's attention on DW and the fireplace, he understands the same fate waits for him.

But being next makes for a much better position than where DW is, getting served to the fire at this very moment.

Another furless cat and the toothless Mother Hamster crouch near the fireplace opening. They grasp the lighter from either side, extending its wick close to the flue. The hamster baby doubling as his mama's tongue crawls onto her back, making it appear as though someone's shoved a wad of chewing gum into her fur. As a result, Mother Hamster works in silence alongside her feline partner.

Two sets of paws attempt the work of one Human hand with an opposable thumb. They push against the black plastic trigger on the lighter. Hiss Honor's curled into an "S," and he scratches a long, pointed tooth against the trigger. It'll take all three working in unison for the *trick* to work.

Try once, click.

Twice, click.

Until the third time, when the yellow flame with a blue heart at its center leaps from the end of the lighter and catches on the invisible gas. There's a whoosh of air getting sucked out and then the fire jumps forward to burn bright in the fireplace. The trio of snake, cat, and hamster fall back in a heap, singed black in spots. The other animals on the hearth gather behind DW. He's crying, screaming, an incoherent mess. But he's fighting against impossible odds and his brain's too broken to find another way out.

Soon enough, it's too late. Soon enough, the scent of burnt fur and flesh melting off tiny bones fills the room. Mingling with the previous noxious gas fumes, the combo's a sickening one. And now's the time when Asher lets it all go.

His bile comes in an arcing spray of red, as though someone's cut his throat. It splatters on the recliner and ricochets back onto those animals holding him fast. The immediate disgust exhibited by those creatures at Asher's inexplicable explosion of sick provides the perfect window of opportunity.

Now's the time when Asher fights full force against those who hold him. He wrenches a shoulder free, then another. He twists and sinks his teeth deep into the face of a young field mouse. He pulls back, spitting out the hunk of the blue-veined ear he's taken with him.

"Restrain him! Restrain him! Bad boy! Bad boy!"

Mr. Muffins screeches his commandments from inside the chest cavity of the Nut House's Death God.

But his words get lost under DW's howling wails from inside the fireplace. For a moment, Asher checks the brick feature to see what's happening. DW's shadow falls across the interior of the hearth, transforming his shade into that of a giant's.

Some ogre engulfed in flames.

Standing on hind legs, DW staggers from the fireplace. He's all lit up and none of the Nut House denizens move to stop him. Forelimbs spread wide, fur sticking up from his head and his entire body covered in a corona of reds and oranges, the burning fox squirrel's shadow reminds Asher of one thing and one thing only…

The tree on fire.

He stares at the squirrel transformed into a stumbling fire. He stares into the flames. He's transfixed in the moment. Outside of this present horror, unfolding and unfolding before his eyes, with each nightmare of sensory input presenting a new fractal version of terror, Asher's pushed deeper and deeper until his present fears connect to memories of fears past.

His legs tense. He's ready to jump. Once more, Asher Black's uncertain what waits for him on the other side.

But I have to jump…

Chapter 6

The Conflagration

No matter how many more moments remain in his life, Asher Black knows he'll never forget the fox squirrel burning. Set ablaze by the Nut House cultists, DW's forward momentum appears to owe more to instinct, the final firing synapses inside his roasting skull, than to any considered purpose. The former consigliere of the Grey Gang lurches from side to side, a glowing monstrosity—more inferno than fur.

Asher stands at attention with his jet-black fur sticking straight up atop his head and in spiked tufts down his back. Flashbacks to his family's tree engulfed in the devastating blaze hold him fast to the spot. His fight or flight's short-circuiting. He's gripped by his certainty that the burning DW's coming for him. The path from the fireplace to Asher's an unavoidable one.

And it's always been that way stretching back to that first fire.

But then, defying the black squirrel's predictions, the fiery fox squirrel pivots. With his forepaws waving from side to side, he instead heads straight for the throng of animals raising ecstatic praises to their Death God. First, yelps and cheeps, then the angry buzzing of insects worshipping She Who Reclines in their alien tongues. Caught in the revelry of singing hosannas to death, the Nut House cultists miss when death comes for them. Whirling, as though made from autumn leaves captured by aggressive breezes, DW's burning body wanders a clumsy, crooked path through the throng of celebrants.

If he falls in a slightly different direction, then one or two of the furry former pets will suffer singed fur, a blistered paw, or a scabrous tail. Minor injuries compared to what's already unfolded in the charnel rooms of the Nut House. But when DW crumbles and surrenders to the flames, he stretches out with his forepaws until his smoky, charred mitts close around the scaled head of the retreating Hiss Honor.

Rasping and spitting, the serpent struggles to break free from the burning squirrel's grasp. However, it's hard to maneuver with the long black wick of the barbecue lighter held between his fanged jaws. As fur and flesh melt into the snake's scales, the fire travels through the melting plastic casing of the lighter. Until the flames reach the fuel hose...

The loud *pop* afterward makes Asher's ears ring and brings black spots floating before his eyes. It's even worse for the screaming Nut House denizens. They're the ones covered in the splattered fiery remnants of DW the fox squirrel and Hiss Honor's head. The rest of the snake writhes and twitches, knocking over smaller mammals trying to flee.

Like raindrops beating against the paved streets, flamelets bounce from one animal's hide to the next. As though the fire's working hard to pet every animal crossing its path. There's a mad scramble for safety, tiny bodies all aglow.

Burning rats seek higher ground and a way out from the conflagration. They scramble up the plastic sheeted loveseat. As the opaque material melts and oozes over their scruffy bodies, the yowling rodents try in vain to reverse course. There are too many of them already on this path. Soon, they're all ablaze and bonded to the plastic sheeting. When they pull back, the cover comes with them. It flies off the loveseat, sending more fire across the living room. The burning plastic, stinking of dead or dying flesh and chemical waste, lands at the foot of the recliner.

Pulling themselves from the sheet, leaving fur, skin, and even limbs behind, the liberated rats stumble toward potential salvation. As the woolen sweater draped over She Who Reclines catches fire, Mr. Muffins digs the claws on his forepaws into the open wound of the corpse's chest. There's a moment of hesitation following, a final reckoning taking place in the piss-yellow eyes of the calico cult leader. As the burning rats scurry inside the chest cavity with him, Mr. Muffins searches for Asher—the final trespasser to be dealt with. He comes up empty and his demeanor changes. The light goes on in his eyes, then off again.

He calls for the other animals in the sing-song voice he's employed so many times before. "Here, babies. It's okay, my precious babies. I'm here for you. Come on up and hug me. Come on, good girls, good boys. That's right..."

The fire paints the room in yellows, reds, and oranges, while also smearing a blue-black layer of smoke across the floor. The Nut House animals obey the voice calling for them. Their brains, broken long before the fire, seek out the words emerging from the corpse of the Human-Female who cared for them, fed them, and sheltered them amid the unfettered excesses of Her suffering mind. As one, they reach the same conclusion: *This is our home.*

Not the Nut House, but the body seated in front of them. Reclining in Her alleged eternal slumber.

Not so eternal anymore...

Mr. Muffins calls the worshippers into the body of their Death God. "Come inside, come inside, there's nothing good outside, my dearies. Come inside!"

Insects fly through or crawl into empty eye sockets. The tiniest mice force wrinkled lips open and fill Her from jaw to gullet. More rats and cats and other pets crawl into the chest cavity. She's aglow with tiny fires everywhere, showing through the sweater layers. Inside the corpse, the animals stay quiet, even as they continue to burn. Their silence is eerie and serene.

Mother Hamster's child-tongue lies inside her mouth, charcoal black and flaking at the touch of her gums rubbing against its head, worrying it away bit by bit.

She waits to swallow and to mourn. Like all the others, she embraces the silence.

It's the silence Asher notices from his position by the front door of the Nut House. The fire travels fast, spread by the junk mail and cardboard littering the floor of the hoarder's nest. Much better than a tree, the home's hoarded treasures and trash prove well suited for the needs of a raging inferno. Plenty of available fuel.

Everything's hot to the touch. Asher waves his forepaws in front of his face, trying to see a few inches ahead. He settles for shadowed impressions and unreliable memories of a place he glimpsed for no more than a few moments earlier in his Nut House ordeal.

Incinerated paint sloughs off the front door and the knob emits a sunburn-pink glow. As Asher swats away another curled finger of smoke before it penetrates too deep into his lungs, he makes an intense study of the burning door. He grabs the sock-made satchel of acorns, pulling it loose to keep melted elastic from sticking to his chest fur. Trembling with adrenaline, he pulls open the sack and scoops out a handful of nuts.

He crunches them between his teeth, fragments of brown shells near-roasted, sticking out every which way from blackened gums. There's a horrible sickly-sweet taste, something not of the trees. It's something that Asher's sure would've killed a squirrel like him in the distant past. But years hidden away in the house, with the whispers in its walls, the cult of a Death God in control, have shifted these poison-soaked shells from affecting the body to warping something deeper inside the black squirrel. Something squirrels, something most animals of Majestic Forest have no word for. With a scream, he drops to all fours by the staircase, then takes off at a sprint, bounding across the burning floor.

He throws his body against the door, right as it's engulfed in flames. After all those years, he's back once again, throwing himself into the fire. When he lands, he rolls across the hardwood revealed by the incinerated debris. He smothers the flames prickling up from his fur as best as he's able.

The heat surrounding him is one thing; but the cool sensations, from additional patches of exposed pink skin revealed after the flames scorch away even more of his black fur, are something else altogether—compelling him forward in this reckless pursuit of freedom.

Another acorn between his teeth, mashed to a pulp, then Asher runs for the door again. Aiming for the same spot, hoping he hasn't inhaled too much smoke and that he's strong enough to weaken the wood further. When he connects this time, his forelimbs spread wide and flames devour the fur from his chest. A chunk of wood comes loose, a blackened burning Human heart-sized lump.

Asher takes it as a sign of progress. There's still a chance for the door to give, allowing him to complete his escape. Even as more and more exposed skin's displayed all over his body, the black squirrel will not relent.

He retreats to the burning staircase, ready for one last run.

As he races toward the door, Asher's bedazzled in crooked crowns of flames. And there's *someone else* behind him.

Chasing him, grabbing at the black squirrel. *She* speaks in hundreds of voices. Mewling, peeping, whining, buzzing, humming. Black flies swarm around eye sockets. Mice tails dangle from wrinkled lips and a calico cat, halfway in and halfway out of a chest cavity, thrusts its burning paws forward.

"There we go! There we go! Pull! Push! Let's move, let's go."

The body of She Who Reclines bulges with animal activity under its skin. Critters pull at bones and muscles, working in tandem to move their Death God forward. They've risen Her from the dead, moved Her to the foyer.

Leaping through black smoke, eyes awash in hot tears sizzling, Asher senses fingertips barely missing the scorched ends of his tail. The brilliant light of the raging fire meets him on the other side of darkness. He slams into the door, hitting the same spot. Again.

He's not alone this time.

A fist covered in rats follows behind him. The door collapses around them, thanks to this follow-through impact. Like a solid object never stood there. Like it was fire all along, masquerading as a door.

Providing the illusion of a door and nothing more.

Fire crackles in Asher's ear. It sounds so close because that's where he's burning. Flames not only travel across the trellises outside the Nut House, consuming the once vibrant green ivy on their way, but they're all over his body as well. The burning's so loud, he misses the birds shrieking in alarm after having their early morning conversations interrupted by this unexpected and unparalleled display of violence. He shakes his head from side to side, but he can't escape the flames and the burning.

His body aches from head to tail. The pain's so intense he also misses the sirens and the flashing lights moseying down the neighborhood streets.

There's no finesse left for the master thief to draw from, no master plan to consult. Survival matters and everything else is an afterthought. Asher Black turns off his mind, setting aside memories already searing their way into his being for all the time he's got left in the world. Avoiding them for the moment, even if he knows it's a losing game, Asher rushes from the Nut House and returns to Majestic Forest.

Even as the burning black squirrel hops and jumps, stretching limbs as far as possible with each movement trailing a brilliant blaze at his back, the Death God, stuffed with Her animal companions turned worshippers, shuffles in his wake. Limbs pop and crack with each creature-controlled motion. Skin burnt blacker than Asher's fur falls to the ground, exploding like puffballs from the trees, casting seeds of fiery death on the grass and cement.

Asher slips between the legs of joggers, while the burning body of She Who Reclines shoves strollers out of its way. The Humans gathering to watch the Nut House burn—*like how the gray squirrels watched the ash tree burn*—are slow to recognize the bizarre and grotesque chase unfolding a few feet away.

They won't accept the idea of animals in control. Witnessing Their bodies desecrated and used for anything other than Their interests and Their pursuits does not compute.

Even as Asher allows himself one glance back over his shoulder to witness the remaining flesh melting from the skull of the Death God, he continues digging his blackened claws into the pavement and pulling forward. His claws crack and split, then bleed. He wonders if the ashes falling from the skull contain the insects or mice who'd hidden inside. He pictures centipedes escaping into the brain, then finding themselves trapped when the flames rose and billowing smoke vomited into the skull smothering everything left inside.

Oakley Grey waits in the one green space left in Majestic Forest, sitting under the oak tree, rubbing his belly. Parkgoers wave, nod, and giggle in his direction. And why not? The jolly, rotund gray squirrel resembles something from Human-Child cartoon fantasies, a drawing of something designed to be loved, cherished, and admired.

A far cry from an ancient past when They drew animals on cave walls to show their respect and fear. The Humans shivered together before the discovery of fire, smearing their feces across cold stone walls to pay homage to the beasts who existed then as more than equals.

When Asher crashes through the hedges surrounding the park and the burning skeletal remains of She Who Reclines come stumbling, stomping after, Oakley has a moment where he experiences the old fears Humans lived through in millennia past. The black squirrel, more black from smoke and his sizzling, charred skin than from any fur left on his body, bounds forward. Eyes gone white, blinded, Asher Black still moves with single-minded purpose.

The shambling skeletal remains of She Who Reclines do the same, even as the last of the Nut House animals burn while clinging to blackened bones.

Asher races at a full sprint, a comet on the ground, getting closer and closer to Oakley. The chubby gray squirrel stands frozen, twitching. His small brain's incapable of processing the unfathomable race heading toward the finish line of *his* tree.

"Mr. Black, Asher, I..."

Piss trickles down his thighs. If squirrels were the praying type, he'd offer up some pleas. But they're not, leaving Oakley with nothing more than an overwhelming urge to live, to keep going day after day. It's a bare minimum for any creature, a standard that appears woefully inadequate to the dangers approaching.

When Oakley throws his forepaws over his face, he's expecting to fend off an attack from an angry, vengeful, burning black squirrel. Instead, there's the slight change in the air as Asher leaps over and past the Grey Gang leader. He crashes through the entryway knot dug into the old oak tree. Then, Asher Black's inside. He burns through the homes of the gray squirrels living under Oakley's protection.

So many of those same squirrels once stood and watched while Asher's home and family burned.

Jittering, shaking Oakley watches smoke pour out of *his* tree. But the faltering footsteps from burnt-up footbones pressing against morning grass slick with dew draw his attention away. Casting his eyes to the heavens, he meets a cat on fire sitting inside the ribcage of a skeleton. "Bad boy! Naughty boy! No treats for you! No treats for you!"

The pathetic scolding from the dying cat is meaningless to the gray squirrel.

And the words make even less sense to those Humans witnessing the horrific tableau. For them, all they pick up are the shrieks of a dying animal—a cat in heat.

Oakley doesn't get a chance to turn away again, once the Death God stumbles to its knees and topples forward. There's a crack like a tree limb breaking off clean from a trunk. Then, the burning skull plummets from the spinal column. Heading for Oakley. As the black sockets and open mouth of the skull come closer, the flames turn upward, making it appear as though he's being greeted by a glowing, radiant grin.

The Humans of Majestic Forest don't appreciate facing too many questions for which no answers appear evident. And yet, after the incident covering the block from the old shut-in's house to the city park one morning in the time between late summer and early autumn, they find themselves burdened with questions and armed with insufficient answers stemming from their limited perspective—above the grass, yet below the trees.

What happened to the old woman?

Must've been some sickos, punks from across town who broke in, and when they didn't find anything worth a damn...they assaulted her, then set her on fire. Can you imagine?

Did you hear about the unpaid bills? Bank was all set to foreclose on her? Inspectors mentioned something about health concerns too...

Oh, the poor, sweet woman.

Not too sweet from what I recall. Mean old bitch. Nasty, too. Bet she killed those animals of hers. Did you hear about all the bones they found?

Breaks my heart thinking about those furry fuzzies oblivious to the dangers in the world. It's why my theory's someone else did it to her...and set those poor critters on fire too.

Animals are our brightest blessing, right?

Things haven't been the same since the squirrels—the gray ones—all ran away. Were you there in the park? Did you see 'em?

They spilled out of the old oak tree. So, so many of them... Not even sure there's anything left in the old tree now.

God, what a horrid thing for kids to witness in broad daylight. No wonder those squirrels left. The poor things must've got traumatized. Do you know if they recovered all of the old lady's skeleton from when it fell? Somebody told me part of it went missing...

How do you even lose something like that?

Well, you wanna know what I think happened?

Asher Black remembers the tree on fire, the house on fire, his friends, enemies, and other incomprehensible beings, all on fire. Inside the oak tree, the blind squirrel lives alone. The gray squirrels and their associates have all fled, giving him the run of the arboreal shelter.

When anyone tries to breach his sanctuary, Asher lashes out from the darkness. So they leave him alone. Because the old oak tree's gone through so much and they'd never dream of cutting it down, what with the backlash they'd encounter.

It's the last original tree in Majestic Forest after all.

Deep in the tree, the blind black squirrel, with his hair growing back in jagged clumps of white—*white of all things*, counts the many acorns he's amassed. Then, he sharpens his teeth on the thick yellow bones of the Death God's skull. The skull he dragged into the oak tree when the gray squirrels ran out, abandoning their home after their leader's demise.

Teeth sharp, eyes blind, fur sparse and white, Asher Black remembers fire. The voices whispering in the branches won't let him forget.

The Acorn Run

A "Nut House" Tale

You think I don't know death? I watched my older brother get eaten whole by a wayward seagull. Frankie: he was one of the fastest gray squirrels I'd ever seen. Could scramble down a tree, dig up an acorn stash, jam 'em all in his cheeks, and rocket back up the trunk before most animals got out a single peep from the lower-lying branches. That was easy for him.

But easy was never what Frankie wanted. He would much rather show off. He was always the one doing a little dance, standing on his back paws, bulging cheeks stuffed full of nutmeat like he was a goddamned chipmunk.

For a seagull blown way, *way* off course, probably traveling farther inland than it'd ever been, all tired and hungry, to come across Frankie making a fool of himself on the forest floor must've seemed like a blessing from the sea.

Damn black-eyed monster, its molting feathers stinking of salt.

I want to tell you I warned Frankie, want to say I screamed his name, or better yet, tell you I ran down and dragged him to safety.

I want a lot of things.

But we're not always so lucky.

I watched as Frankie met that white-feathered head and the gaping maw, opening wider, wider, and wider still. Then, the bird tossed its head back and Frankie lost any chance he might've had to run. Soon, his back paws and tail were twitching, while the rest of him slid down that seagull's gullet.

A sharp cracking sound followed, likely the bird flexing and breaking my brother's neck. A mercy for Frankie, but not so much for me. The noise woke up every other critter that called the oak home.

They were chittering and chirping, roaring and screaming, all at once. Frankie's death brought us together. It might've been the last thing that did. The damn bird looked up at the oak, confused as to how a whole tree could get so mad at it. Stomach sagging, it flapped once, twice, then got off the ground and flew away between the trees.

And that was that.

At least as far as my brother and the bird were concerned. Me? I wasn't so lucky.

You see, Frankie had done something very, very bad. The acorn stashes under the oak weren't meant to be touched, not until the colder months. Violating that rule was bad enough. But then you throw in whose stash it was that he'd ripped off…jamming the acorns in his cheeks, cheeks that were now being digested in the guts of a seabird?

Those nuts belonged to the fox squirrels.

Reynard was the leader of the fox squirrels and the scariest animal living in our oak tree at the time. Not ugly-scary though. Far from it, Monsieur Reynard, as he preferred to be called, was quite the representative of his kind. His fur was sleek, almost wet looking. He smelled of pine, despite living in the oak. Had long ears, and a long body, too. He had an intimidating presence, I believe you'd call it.

And he wasn't violent-scary either. Not like a mad dog foaming at the mouth or raccoons that'll corner victims and rip out their guts. That's not to say Reynard didn't have the capacity for violence. He most certainly did.

But he worked under cover of darkness, a ruthlessly efficient executioner. If a critter crossed him, they'd be fine during the day, then night would come and they'd be gone by the time the sun rose at dawn.

Some of the older gray squirrels, my uncles, would joke that Reynard had actual fox lineage in his blood. Papa never stood for that talk though, so I only heard those quips when he wasn't around.

Papa was a good squirrel, a squirrel who believed in all the talk about us animals working and living together. Though, *believed* might be too strong a word. Call it *hoped for*.

Because he recognized when threats were present and dangers were real. Losing the fox squirrels' stash had made us grays their number-one enemy. With the actual culprit gone—quite literally—to the heavens, the blame fell on Frankie's family. That meant Papa and it also meant me. We became the targets of the fox squirrels' wrath.

Suddenly, I'd become the heir apparent to an empire. Me, the timid one. The one who hid under leaves on the forest floor, who'd dig deeper and deeper at the first whiff of danger, until I'd get all turned around under the leaf cover, unable to figure out which ways were up, down, or sideways. In those moments of panic, I'd scream and cry and my big brother would have to dive into the hole I'd made, dragging me back to the surface, where Papa was waiting, shaking his head.

No more rescuing for me though. Frankie was dead and I'd moved up, the next in line. It was easy to see that development didn't sit well with Papa.

He called me to near the top of the oak, a place hidden amid a tangle of leaf-filled branches. I was scared just climbing up there. The whole time I was climbing, one paw in front of the other, I imagined what Papa would have to say, how he'd dress me down in front of the uncles, what names he'd call me.

I suppose having those familial fears running through my brain helped in the long run because they gave me something to pass the time with, while I made steady progress upward. By the time I reached Papa's branches and found the five fox squirrels balanced on limbs to either side of my path, three on one side and two on the other, I was numb with self-inflicted anxiety. A little more fear didn't matter all that much.

Papa waited on a separate branch, with Monsieur Reynard beside him. Both their tails were held stiff and at attention, both their noses wrinkled, sniffing the air with unmistakable insistence. It was clear neither trusted the other. *But what could I even do about that?* I remember thinking.

Before I found an answer, Papa filled me in on the mission. The *job*. Call it what you like. For me, the lone gray squirrel going out on a search-and-recovery mission with a bunch of pissed-off fox squirrels, there was only one thing I knew to call it: a death sentence.

"Outside of this forest, They've started building dens. Monsieur Reynard and his fox squirrels here have had spies...sorry, scouts...scouts out, keeping tabs on things, seeing what They're doing, how They're trying to live.

"I must begrudgingly offer compliments on this foresight. I would've hoped Monsieur Reynard and his cohort might share this intelligence with all of us oak-tree denizens.

"But you and your brother have made sure certain such alliances are delayed for the moment. Yes, for the foreseeable future, at least.

"Lucky for us—and you—an exception has presented itself. We have an opportunity to move along the path to reconciliation and continued coexistence. Call it a matter of convenience. First, the fox squirrels have lost their cache for winter. While I've offered to share from our stores, pride—well that is how I see it at least—prevents our cousins from accepting what they deem 'charity.' Instead, they've identified an alternative source for acorns that would serve as an adequate replacement for what was lost.

"It would seem They...have false trees outside a number of their dwellings, trees meant to lure birds and our kind...and each contains a rich bounty of seeds and nuts. That is the rumor at least.

"A group of the fox squirrels will leave the forest, venture to those 'nests,' and return with the bounty. You will accompany them, serving as the representative of the gray squirrels. For this year, the fox squirrels alone will enjoy the fruits of this labor, but you will mark the location and the best path to reach it. That way both fox and gray squirrels will possess this knowledge and neither group will have an advantage over the other."

Papa was long-winded by nature and design. Mama would say he'd achieved power within the gray squirrel ranks by talking his way into it, refusing to cede the floor once he'd started. Eventually, any challengers would tire of waiting, hoping in vain to get a word in edgewise. "Monsieur Reynard will accompany you and his crew. He is aware of the consequences should any harm befall you."

The elder fox squirrel smiled, cheeks pulled back to show jagged teeth like broken rocks. "Not to worry, Grey," Reynard said, addressing Papa but keeping his blackened eyes on me. "We'll take good care of him."

I gripped the thin branch I balanced on even tighter, worrying I'd pass out and plummet to the forest floor. I couldn't believe Papa would subject his heir to such a likely trap. Despite his professed confidence in my safety, as some bargaining chip to keep the peace, the opportunity for revenge from the fox squirrels seemed too perfect. It certainly wasn't something that Frankie would've passed up.

"Don't worry, little pup," Reynard said, seemingly reading my mind. "If we wanted to kill you, we'd do it here and now."

I looked to Papa, hoping he'd speak out against the implied threat. But he stared over my head and out through the branches, maybe contemplating the shapes of clouds or the color of the sky.

"Are you gonna cling to this trunk your whole life, scared of your shadow beneath the light of the sun? Burrowing under dead leaves and hiding from the world?"

Frankie had a way with words. Where Papa was verbose, my big brother was selective and incisive when speaking. He especially knew how to cut me to the quick. Those questions were the last words he shared, before diving down the oak on that final fatal acorn run.

I was supposed to be the one stealing from the fox squirrels. He'd dared me to grab a nut—one single, solitary nut—and race back up to a branch where he'd be waiting. No squirrel or other critter in the oak should've even known we'd gone into the fox squirrels' cache. For Frankie, everything was a test, an initiation ritual. Throughout my life, he'd set a relentless series of obstacles in my path because…because he'd been there first, I suppose. In a way him dying was one more challenge laid out before me.

Where my family used words to great effect, the fox squirrels took a completely different approach, wielding their silences with purpose. Us gray squirrels, we're a chatty bunch when we're on the move. And we're always on the move.

Leaping through the branches, scurrying across the ground, loading our cheeks with nuts and paws with twigs, chittering and chattering is a natural state of being no matter the activity.

But when this exploratory group departed the next morning, me plus four fox squirrel lieutenants and their big boss, I suppressed any urge to chirp and chortle. The fox squirrels led the way, their slightly larger, sleeker bodies allowing them to cover more ground so they were running ahead the whole time. Their big boss and I brought up the rear of our party.

Even though Reynard stayed by my side the entire trip, as the others zigged and zagged and looped around and up and back again, somehow, some way, I felt surrounded, with every bounding leap I took, every scramble to hold onto a branch, every swing and swish of my tail. The others moved so quickly, so silently, so efficiently, I could imagine them doubling back and sneaking up on me, before rushing forward once again. It was the sort of game that Frankie would've liked to play.

Only Monsieur Reynard kept pace with me. Never speeding up, never slowing down. He didn't follow fox squirrel custom and instead maintained a steady dialogue, though given its one-sided nature I suppose it would've been better classified as monologue. While we made our way through the forest, he told a story. A portion of a story actually. Something a bit like an acorn. Experiencing the story in its compact form, I could imagine something greater, more permanent waiting to burst forth from its hard shell. Not in the moment, but many years later. Isn't that what stories are? Seeds for more stories?

"Do you know the story of the squirrel who thought he was a Man?" Reynard asked me.

"I see you shaking your head. Don't think I don't notice. I always see what I need to out here in the forest, young Grey.

"Are you afraid because I use Their word—Man?

"Don't be. They believe They have power over us because They have words, names for things. They believe They rule because They can call us things but we do not call Them anything in return.

"Do you understand? No? That is okay. Perhaps you will in time.

"Long ago, before Man was Man and kept himself separate from the rest of the critters, back when he wore our skins and not the strange lifeless things devoid of fur and heft and heat that he slithers into today, like some snake and not our giant furless cousin, missing a tail to swing with or teeth suitable for cracking nuts, a squirrel decided he would rather become a Man.

"I cannot say if it was a gray or a fox or some other squirrel, some ancient ancestor from which both our tribes are descended. Accept that it was a squirrel, just as you are accepting that this is a story I am telling you.

"This squirrel hid in the branches. He peeked from behind tree trunks or out from under the exposed roots of the trees in the forest, studying Man with every passing moment. Neglecting food-gathering, leaving his mate alone in their tree, barren in every sense. He devoted himself fiendishly, feverishly to memorizing every motion and utterance of the critter called Man. He mimicked their motions, their sounds, until he could walk among his fellow forest critters striding tall—for a squirrel at least—and proud, on two limbs rather than four, moving his head with slow, steady purpose. The way a Man would.

"Soon, that squirrel began to see the forest and its inhabitants the way Man does. All other critters were viewed as either foes or food. He lashed out at weaker ones, knocking them from branches, leaving their bodies broken on the forest floor below him. He gnawed off ears, left victims bloody and senseless in the wake of his attacks. Often, he'd leave the killing job unfinished, refusing to grant these critters the mercy of death. He claimed to be following the way of Man.

"Finally, the other critters had enough and formed a united opposition, standing against the squirrel who wanted to be a Man. They refused him entry into any tree, any hole, or any hovel. There was no woodland sanctuary left for the squirrel.

"And, oh, how he howled and raged when faced with their denials and resistance. Because he was a Man or wanted to be one at the very least. Man would never apologize. Man would never repent, never beg forgiveness for past misdeeds committed against beings he viewed as his lessors. Man would take and take, because all Man knows is indulgence.

"Imagine, young gray squirrel, one of our kind carrying on louder than a bear or bobcat, louder than the seven-spring cicada. This calamity echoed off the trees in the forest that day. This temper tantrum drew an audience.

"Men. A Man and his whelp. Pale, wormy-fleshed creatures. Not even the most remarkable or intimidating of their kind. This Man-child gaped at the sight of the mad squirrel. Then, his elder placed a hand on the offspring's shoulder and gave a nod. At that point, they raised their sticks and made fire and thunder explode from them, and the squirrel who wanted to be a Man was left as a smear of blood, autumnal leaf reds and the pink of summer sunsets, splashed across the forest floor.

"The Man-child pulled the squirrel's tail out from the bloody remains, pinching it between two digits on his forepaws. Swinging it back and forth. Laughing, chittering with excitement. He ran ahead, deeper into the forest, leaving the carnage in which he had partaken.

"We're here."

The fox squirrel's final comment left me confused and disoriented. I'd become so engrossed in his tale, even while a tiny part shouted inside that it was nothing more than a fable, a warning shared with superstitious critters. Regardless, it was an entrancing telling. At last, I realized he had finished his tale and the *here* he referred to was the end of the forest and the beginning of Their territory.

The heat. That's the first thing you notice about Their land. They cut down trees, covering the ground and the water alike. Everything is dry, hard, dead. Papa once told me and Frankie, "They make a skeleton atop the earth wherever they go, showing us the rot happening below."

It's one of the better explanations for the process that I've ever heard.

At that moment, I witnessed Their desolation first-paw. Strange to say, I was grateful to not be alone in the experience. All of us squirrels stood at the ragged edge, the final grasslands separating our world from Theirs. Myself and five fox squirrels, none of us moving. I looked down our line, waiting to see who'd slide their paw forward first, who'd test their limbs on that too-solid gray and black ground They'd spread like sickness before us.

All the fox squirrel lieutenants trembled as I did. Even those who'd participated in previous scouting expeditions into Their territory. I even caught the shivering fear making its presence known in Monsieur Reynard himself.

But he caught me looking, saw me absorbing his fear, taking it inside. A look of recognition passed between us, his acknowledgment of my possession—the memory of his terror. It was the absolute worst thing that could have happened.

Once a leader knows his fear has been witnessed and will be remembered, every desperate action taken after is done in service of making you forget what you've seen. The vain illusory hope that it will all just disappear.

"What do you mean you want to leave the oak?"

That question started it all, setting me off on a suicide mission of an acorn run. A run I've been making—one way or another—ever since.

As soon as I'd asked the question, Frankie's forepaws were up in my face, covering my mouth, his claws scratching at my cheeks. I sputtered and coughed, preparing to scream. But "Shhh," he said, "shhh, shhh, shh. You wanna wake the whole tree?"

I quieted myself. I'd been criticized for my habit of hiding, but there was at least one skill the practice had helped me to hone, one strength: I could stay still, stay silent, and listen.

I waited for Frankie to speak.

It took a bit, but he finally broke. He hopped to the branch above me, scrambling back and forth on the limb, chittering away the whole time. It was easy enough to recognize what he was doing. I'd seen it before big acorn runs or brawls with the wilder chipmunks or the rats—those nasty ground-dwellers who'd grown bolder and more savage in their assaults as They encroached on the land.

Still, I waited him out on the branch below. At last, Frankie dug the claws of his forepaws into the trunk and swung down, his head facing me and his tail swishing against the branch above.

"I don't wanna be the leader, kid," he said. "I ain't cut out for the life. Not like Pops is. Not like y—"

"But that's the way it's always been," I said, cutting him off, not wanting the conversation to go any further. "The oldest becomes the leader of the gray squirrels. It's your birthright."

Frankie shifted, switching positions against the trunk so his head was now aimed toward the top of the tree and his tail was swishing down against my face. I bristled at this contact, though looking back I don't believe it was a malicious gesture.

Not intentionally so.

"I've been doing a lot of climbing, ya know?" he asked.

I nodded, not sure if he saw, not sure if it mattered.

"I climbed past the upper branches, past where Pops conducts business. I know you don't like going up there, but it ain't too bad. Trick's to never look down. But I've been going higher than that even. To the very top.

"A couple of times, I've even jumped. You really gotta push, but if you get the leg strength and the wind's right, you can make it to one of the pines.

"Then, you wanna talk climbing? Forget about it. You get up to the top of the pines and you can see almost anything, *everything*. Real ornery birds up there. But the view...

"I think I could see to the end of the earth."

Staring at Monsieur Reynard's body exploded across the tarry ground, with curling wisps of steam rising from the pink and gray mush of his remains, I considered whether or not I might've had a death curse attached to me. Not a direct one, but one that rubbed off on others. Anyone who got too close. Between swallowed Frankie and the flattened fox squirrel, there was plenty of evidence to support it.

Reynard had leaped into the black without a sound, not indulging in a grandiose battle cry. He'd jumped but hadn't checked if the coast was clear. The screaming beast, the armored shell They wear sometimes like giant scuttling insects, stampeded over him. Like he was nothing at all.

It didn't slow down. Didn't stop to sniff its kill. Somehow roaring and squealing all at once, it left the fox squirrel to spray bloody berries from his lips instead of last words.

Taking in the bloody scene before me, my hind paws gave out. That was it as far as I was concerned. Any hope I had of survival was splattered across Their "road."

I closed my eyes, hiding from the forever foggy, forever open eyes of Reynard.

Don't close your eyes, dummy.

I heard Frankie.

It was good advice. I opened my eyes in time to catch the slashing fox squirrel claw coming for my face. The claw in question belonged to one of Reynard's lieutenants, one with part of his left ear chewed away and irritated, bloodshot eyes glowing red. Volpe was his name. I leaped back from the attack but slammed against two of the other fox squirrels instead. Those two were brothers. Brown and Little their nicknames.

They were gray-furred, close to black, and huge. Before I could squirm free they'd wrapped their thick limbs around me, holding me tight against their beefy bodies. One of the brothers snapped at me, taking a bite from my cheek. Not a nip, this was a deep enough wound to pull flesh and fur away. I howled in pain.

I still carry the scar today.

Before Volpe could try to slash me again or one of the brothers could take another bite, I found my voice. "Wait!" I cried. "Wait! Please, just...wait!"

It wasn't the Brothers or Volpe who spoke next. It was the other one, the fourth underling, clearing his throat, who growled his retort.

Todd. That's what they called him. Strange name, but one I wasn't likely to forget. "Tell us, little Grey-Pup," he said, slotting himself into the leadership position just like that, "tell us, why we shouldn't hold you out there in the black and wait for Them to treat you like they did Monsieur Reynard?"

It was a damn good question.

It required an answer that wouldn't get me killed. One that would keep me around a little longer. Frankie wouldn't have worried. He'd have spat the first vile words that came to mind.

But Frankie's dead and you're still alive.

The other fox squirrels let me go. While they gave me space to catch my breath and consider my response, they remained close at paw, no doubt ready to make good on previous threats. I lifted a paw to my lips and wiped away drool. My cheeks were damp, tears spilling from my eyes. The sun was bright, almost unbearably bright, with little tree cover and that black earth reflecting the rays onto us.

But none of it mattered.

You see I'd waited, I'd considered, and even contemplated, until an answer came. I'd found a way I could make myself useful, buy myself more time among the living.

"I'll carry the nuts!"

Todd, the new fox squirrel leader, leaned closer following my exclamation. His expression fell somewhere between a smirk and an inquisitive raised brow.

"What's that Grey-pup?" he asked.

"I'll carry everything. You'll all be free and clear. You'll be the heroes of the fox squirrels, heroes of the oak even. Carrying on in the event of a tragedy. And all you have to do is make sure we *all* make it home."

That smirk deepened across Todd's face and spread to his fellows. I held my breath, the ground shaking under my paws.

Strange to think, but it was a relief when more of Them passed over the blackened earth, hardened shells vibrating and pushing hot air against our furry faces. When They were gone, Todd gave a nod, my reprieve granted. We continued searching for the acorns.

Papa never spoke about the time before the fox squirrels lived in the oak. Or perhaps it's better to say he never talked much about it to me.

Frankie? Oh, Frankie heard plenty. And he'd whisper the stories to me, especially when I was a pup, so scared of my own shadow. Tales of turf wars. Bloody battles fought in the branches. Squirrels scratching, tearing, biting across the forest. Acorn caches destroyed. Pink, mewling newborns thrown from nests or given to dead-eyed birds to devour.

The stuff of nightmares.

"Papa once destroyed a whole nest of newborn fox squirrels. By himself," Frankie told me one time.

My eyes grew wide. I was certain they'd pop from my skull and spill on the forest floor like discarded nutshells. I imagined another squirrel burying my eyes, and I welcomed the notion. Not that it mattered. The visuals Frankie provided still thrived in my head.

His laughter cut my doom-visioning short.

"Who would you kill to keep us safe? Who wouldn't you kill even?"

His questions hung heavy between us. At first, I thought he was joking, pushing my buttons as he loved to do. But he kept waiting for an answer. Claws scratched at the wood of the oak, shredding its leaves. I soon realized he was expecting a response.

We found the dwelling. Or perhaps it's better to say that it found us.

Looming over us, a tired, bedraggled gang of squirrels, it was incomplete, a skeleton. It stood among others of its ilk. Those nests were in various stages of completion. This dwelling had "branches" intersecting at an angle. Slatted and smooth, the wood from our trees, repurposed in death.

By that point in our mission, my limbs ached. The remaining fox squirrels had pushed me harder, faster, farther. Whether luck or destiny or ill fate, every "feeder" we tried was barren. No seeds, no nuts. The supposed bounty was picked over by birds or scavenger squirrels living in town, gazing from the shadows of the few trees They retained near Their homes.

Still, with each feeder, the fox squirrels would order me up the skinny trunk of the lifeless structure to perform reconnaissance.

Then, I'd come back, relaying more disappointing news. The fox squirrels would jeer and hiss, cuffing me in the scruff behind my head. With no fruitful rewards to show for this labor, I grew more and more certain that my time among the living critters was coming to an end.

That skeletal dwelling changed everything. It was something new. Something different.

"Oi! Where do you think you're going?" Volpe the fox squirrel asked. He'd grabbed my forelimb, pinching through the fur. His claws gouged so deep I worried he'd scratch bone.

"I think there's something up there," I said. I wasn't thinking too deeply about my words, just letting them come.

Like Frankie would've.

"What do you mean?" one of the twins asked. "You're talking crazy."

"No, let's give the pup a chance," Todd said. I found no mercy in his tone, nothing like I'd heard from the departed Monsieur Reynard. Todd's words dripped cruelty off every syllable.

He wanted me to fail. Needed an excuse for them to tear me limb from limb. I imagined Todd, Volpe, Brown, and Little, leaving my corpse inside Their dwelling.

But I knew I was right. I *knew* there was something up there.

I scampered across the dirt, weaving between thin sprouts of green grass rising from the overturned earth. The fox squirrels ran behind me. Based on their caution, I could tell they had never been around one of Their dwellings in such an unfinished state either. It was so...open. Not closed up, isolated like the completed versions tend to be. Wanting nothing to do with the world around them. There was something, at once, inviting and foreboding about this difference.

Horseflies buzzed in a chorus rising and falling. Those fat black bugs dive-bombed us as we got closer to the structure. They got so bad, we all stopped and covered our heads. Waiting for the miniature dark cloud to pass us by.

I might've considered their presence an omen. Some warning. But I was tired, too scared of the real and the tangible dangers before me and behind me to care.

"When I'm gone I want to see you come into your own, little brother."

"You won't see anything, Frankie. You'll be dead."

"Is that so? Well, maybe you'll see me then."

"I don't think..."

"That's a good start, little brother. Don't think. It'll take you far. Don't think until you have to."

Here's the first secret of this tale I'm sharing. I don't know where the acorns came from. I know what critters say. I know that dwelling is supposed to be where I *hid* the nuts, nuts I'd already found. Nuts I'd taken from the fox squirrels even. Like I tricked or outsmarted them somehow. It's fine, I suppose, if that's what critters want to believe. Truth be told, I've sometimes found myself believing that version of events. But deep inside, I know it's not the *true* version of what happened on that acorn run.

Truth is…I don't know where the acorns came from. They were already there. A huge pile of golden-brown nuts, all plump and shiny, like they were freshly fallen from another oak, somewhere out there. The pile sat balanced on a cross-section of the cold, wooden "ribs" of Their dwelling.

Like an offering.

I salivated, seeing them, inhaling the woodland fragrance their little caps gave off. A natural enough response considering what was presented to me. To us.

Because there was much more than one winter's cache there. There were enough acorns to feed the oak critters ten times over. A generational stash.

The fox squirrels called up to me from the base of the dwelling, their claws scratching at a hard gray surface planted over the muddy earth. I think They call it a *floor*. "What you got, pup? You hiding up there?"

The spittle dried in my mouth. Worn out, depleted, and starving, but my hunger came to heel. There were greater needs that needed tending to.

"It's…it's…"

I waved my forepaws, trying to block the vision materializing before my eyes. At the apex of the skeletal structure, I saw the seagull hovering in mid-flight. It was the same one I'd watched swallow my brother whole. It flapped its dirty salt-stained wings hard and fast. But they made no sound and pushed no air across my face. In a silent scream, the bird's beak hung down, opened wide. Wider than it should have been. And there was Frankie, drenched in blood and stomach juices, fur gone from half his face so I could see the meat and bone beneath, reaching for me, crawling from the bird's mouth. His forepaws waved back at me. Wet fur pressed against bone and muscle, he screeched in silence from within his devourer's silent shriek. An echoing omen, undeniable this time.

But I still didn't want to know what Frankie and the seagull had to say, what warning they wished to convey. My only interest was in making them go away.

Yet the fox squirrels took my frantic hand motions as a signal—a sign that they were needed. Soon, those other four critters were clambering the structure, moving to join me at the top. When they arrived, the hallucinatory incarnations of Frankie and the killer bird were gone. There was only me, a tired, scared, runt of a gray squirrel and a bigger pile of acorns than any of us critters had ever seen all at once.

The fox squirrel foursome laughed, long and loud, the raucous sound echoing off the smooth, lifeless wood. "Good going, pup!" Todd said. He scooped up two of the acorns, so shiny and fresh, practically dripping with golden moisture. His tongue flicked out from his mouth, to caress the hardened shell.

Brown and Little took things further, smashing their pilfered nuts against the skeletal planks. I watched their paws scooping the meat out, shoving it into their greedy maws.

"Hey, hey, you think we should be eating these? Shouldn't we load that pup up to take 'em to the nest?" Volpe asked, seemingly the lone voice of sanity amid his acorn-mad peers.

Todd quit nibbling on the acorn gripped between his paws. He set it down gently. Little and Brown followed his lead. I tensed.

I *knew* who I was. I knew I was no fighter. Not like Frankie had been. Four on one would be overkill, but it'd also be a death sentence all the same. My eyes darted, searching for a path of escape. Seeking somewhere to hide.

"Look, Volpe," Todd spoke, interrupting my already frenzied thought processes, "with this many acorns, we don't just have enough for the fox squirrels back home. No, no, no…"

"What do you mean?" one of the big ones asked. Let's say it was Brown.

"What I mean is…this is the sort of cache you start an *empire* with. We bring these back home and the days of the gray squirrels running things are over. We'll control the nuts going in, out, and falling from the oak. How's that sound, fellas?"

"Sounds good, boss," the other big one, Little, said.

None of it sounded good to me. My stomach rumbled, not just from hunger and exhaustion any longer. Fear reasserted itself as well.

Todd continued. "Seems to me the four of us can carry these nuts back to *our* home all by ourselves. Seems to me, like, maybe we don't need the help no more. What do you say, pup?"

But I was already gone, leaping away with those final syllables. Scampering across the skeletal structure, racing down those rib-like beams. My heart pounded in my ears. My tail stuck out stiff and straight behind me.

The thundering clatter of fox squirrel claws echoed at my back. They were coming. I turned a corner, bouncing between the slatted beams. One claw chipped when it jammed into the smooth, lifeless wood the wrong way. I felt myself tipping over, ready to fall.

But I righted and kept on running. I wouldn't risk a look behind. I wasn't as fast as Frankie. I couldn't lose the time it'd take to see if they followed.

Up ahead, the dwelling revealed itself to be more complete than the initial impression we'd received. A pink cottony substance stretched across the back. I looked down through the dead, slatted wood and saw fat rolls of the pink substance, waiting on Their floor below me. Waiting to be put to use. It was easy enough to figure it for nesting materials, a layer of protection around the skeleton. Just as the seagull's feathers helped give it form and our fur gives us squirrels our shape, our definition.

For the moment, though, that fuzzy substance represented one and one thing only to me: a place to hide.

After Papa tried to eat me, after I'd hid below the oak, burying myself beneath a pile of dead leaves, feeling as discarded by the oak as they were, Frankie found me first. But he didn't pull me out, didn't drag me into the dim tree-cover-shaded sun. Not at once.

Instead, he pushed leaves and twigs aside, widening the hole I'd carved through the forest debris to accommodate his additional mass. He pressed his body against me. I must have tried to squirm away. But he draped his forepaws over my shoulders and pulled me to him.

I felt his breath, hot along the inner folds of my ear.

"It's okay to hide," he said. "Just make sure that when you stop hiding, you come out with a plan for how you'll fight back."

The strangled cries of the four fox squirrels reached my hiding place behind the pink substance delineating where Their walls would later be placed. The squirrels themselves were not so lucky in their quest to find me.

Claws broke through the pale pink border of my secret location. I scooted back, moving deeper inside the fuzzy and scratchy substance. I stopped once I realized the flailing paws weren't moving with intention. Nor malice. There was a desperate, flailing quality to their movement.

Instead of intelligible cries, the fox squirrels' exclamations emerged as gurgles and chirps. A long guttural howl, wet and aspirating with blood, greeted my ears. I crawled closer, traveling back through the pink to the borders of the skeletal frame. I promised to stay hidden but refused to stay in the dark regarding what was happening to my would-be executioners.

Finally, a paw's-length away from exiting seclusion, I saw bright red speckling dotting the pink. Then, closer still, deep crimson puddles made the pink fuzz sag along its wooden bones. I heard the words of one of the squirrels. Volpe I think. They passed as an exasperated whisper, dripping with sadness and frustration over some cruel and unexpected twist of fate.

"The acorns..."

Volpe and the other fox squirrels collapsed one after the other after the other after the other.

Until, finally, there was a silence settling into the bones of the dwelling. Confronted with this new companion, I thought about my brother's face, my father's as well. I saw another face. Something white and skeletal. Burning. I felt flames under my skin, growing more and more intense so I soon feared I'd have to tear through fur and flesh to unlock the blazing inferno.

I cast aside my apocalyptic sensations, and pushed ahead, emerging from the pink walls, as if I'd undergone a second birth.

Death waited for me, in the form of four dead fox squirrels laid across the ribs of the dwelling. White foaming spittle oozed from the corners of their slackened mouths. Vomited chunks of poison-laced nut meat splattered from them, dripping to the floor below.

I recalled the words of my brother. The direction he'd given me, the knowledge he'd passed before his demise.

Only, I didn't have a plan for how to fight back. Not in that moment. I realized I needed to remain hidden, if not physically, then perhaps spiritually. Not only me but the four dead fox squirrels and the poisoned cache of acorns as well.

The work of hiding everything took a long time. I moved acorns one or two at a time, keeping them tucked between my forepaw and upper body rather than stuffed in my mouth. Then, once the cache was secreted away behind that pink substance, I turned my attention to the foursome. By the time I got to them, their bodies were stiff and cold. There was no give as I dragged their corpses over the wood. One of the big ones twisted at an unexpected and unnatural angle and I heard the *pop* of his neck bones once I yanked hard enough to get him back on track.

When my work was finished, I considered staying up there at the top of the dwelling, waiting for the house to be built up around me. I pictured the home as a den for animals and for death, both in equal measure. I'm not sure where this thought came from. Like my earlier vision of the burning skeleton, I felt touched by another presence in the emptiness of the dwelling. I felt a greater beast than myself or any other critter I'd ever encountered. I knew that if I stayed, I'd live on borrowed time. Sooner or later, this Other, this being who'd claimed the dwelling for its own, would grow tired or hungry and I would be destroyed or devoured.

One paw in front of the other, I crawled to the ground and made my run through the darkened desolation of Their portion of the world. The artificial suns hanging from the fake metal trees lit my path, guiding my return to the forest's edge. I ran fast, as fast as I possibly could. That last run was my tribute to Frankie. I ran for my brother and the future that we were both denied. I left the fox squirrels and the poisoned acorns behind in Their dwelling, hidden. They would have a role to play there. Their purpose became clear to me, under the false light as I ran across Their dead, black earth.

The last part of my plan revealed itself at the forest's edge. There, where the light ended and the dark reclaimed its natural supremacy. I stopped at the edge of Their ebony earth. My claws came just shy of dipping into the thick, congealing blood of the now long-dead Monsieur Reynard. They had left him there still, even after all our time on the hunt for the bounty. Only the flies and their maggot offspring had seen fit to pay a visit. They buzzed heavy, skimming over the puddled gore. Their droning helped to cover my scream, a shrill cry as much of terror as relief. Letting it all out at once, hollowing myself. Preparing for what I needed to do next.

When I stopped screaming, the flies remained, unphased. They zipped around me and the corpse pieces littering the ground. They didn't care which of us squirrels was alive or which was dead. We were all the same.

We were all the same.

So now, here's one more secret for you. But you're a smart critter, so I suspect you've already figured it out.

When the leader of the gray squirrels, my Papa, was attacked by a returning and blood-mad Monsieur Reynard, the fox squirrel leader who was said to have declared a vendetta against the grays, do you know who wore the old fox's skin and fur, who hid inside the other critter's skin, and who let the dark blood dribble down his eyes and mouth, a mouth already filled with buzzing, vibrating flies heavy with serum? Can you guess who hid inside Reynard?

You know, don't you?

Of course, that's not the story we tell the gray squirrels who rule the oak tree now. The story we tell has me emerging from a hiding place outside the oak, rushing to help my father tear the attacking Reynard apart. But when we've finished with him, it's too late for Papa and he succumbs to the fox-squirrel-inflicted wounds. His rightpaw squirrels, rushing up the tree, find me, waiting out in the open air. The leaders of the gray squirrels and the fox squirrels are beside me, dead.

But not me. I am alive. I am not hiding

No, I'm never hiding again.

Acknowledgements

It's funny how books like this one you're holding in your hand (or on your electronic device of choice) can have a long (and bushy!) tail from conception to final iteration. That is most certainly true for *The Nut House*. To take a project on a journey of that nature involves a lot of people signing onto the vision and helping to make it realized.

First and foremost, thanks to Charles Tyra of *Cosmic Horror Monthly* fame for connecting with the initial pitch to have a story about squirrels serialized in his magazine. Having that first door open to the project has led us down the path to this final destination.

And my thanks to Eliza Broadbent for providing the connection to the fine folks at Undertaker Books, thus setting up the next stage in the life of Asher and company.

Speaking of Undertaker, I must thank D.L. Winchester and Cyan LeBlanc for taking the chance on this talking-animal/crime/cosmic horror hybrid and embracing the vision I had for the book version. Special thanks to Rebecca Cuthbert, a wonderful writer and an attentive editor, who's been the point person for the metamorphosis of *The Nut House* to book form.

One of the things that I really wanted for the book was to have a strong visual element, giving readers who'd already experienced Asher's adventures in serialized form that little something extra. JC Amberlyn's interior illustrations and Dakota Marquardt's brilliant cover were both more than ready to meet this challenge. Both capture the look and feel of the world I wanted to share with readers.

Thanks to those who've supported this weird project from the get-go. Readers like Tim Bloom and Matt Brandenburg who responded to the initial version of the project with such enthusiasm helped me to see that "Hey! there might be a little something more here." It should go without saying, but I'll say it anyway, that the endorsements of Paul Michael Anderson and Pauline Chow are treasured by your humble author here. They're both dear friends and writers I admire, and being able to find folks that fall into both those categories is one of the highlights of this writing journey. I also want to thank Chloe York, a fellow Undertaker author, for taking the time to read the book and share her generous endorsement.

Finally, thanks to the usual suspects. Jenna, Grant, and Avery: you always surprise me and my love for you has no limits.

Publication History

The Nut House was originally serialized in six parts in *Cosmic Horror Monthly*.

Publication History of The Nut House:

"The Crew" appeared in *Cosmic Horror Monthly #25*, July 2022

"The Cache" appeared in *Cosmic Horror Monthly #26*, August 2022

"The Coward" appeared in *Cosmic Horror Monthly #27*, September 2022

"The Creep" appeared in *Cosmic Horror Monthly #28*, October 2022

"The Corpse" appeared in *Cosmic Horror Monthly #29*, November 2022

"The Conflagration" appeared in *Cosmic Horror Monthly #30*, December 2022

"The Acorn Run: A 'Nut House' Tale" is original to this volume.

For more information on *Cosmic Horror Monthly*, check out: cosmichorrormonthly.com

Coming Soon

La Casa de las Nuestras, Spanish translated edition of *The Nut House*,
Dimensiones Ocultas

About the Author

Patrick Barb is an author of weird, dark, and spooky tales, currently living (and trying not to freeze to death) in Saint Paul, Minnesota. His recently published works include the dark fiction collections *The Children's Horror* and *Pre-Approved for Haunting*, the novellas *JK-LOL* and *Night of the Witch-Hunter*, as well as the novelette *Helicopter Parenting in the Age of Drone Warfare*. He is the editor and publisher of the anthology *And One Day We Will Die: Strange Stories Inspired by the Music of Neutral Milk Hotel*. His debut sci-fi/horror novel *Abducted* is coming from Dark Matter Ink in late 2025. His 2023 short story "The Scare Groom" was selected for *Best Horror of the Year Volume 16*.

Visit him at patrickbarb.com.

About the Illustrator

JC Amberlyn is an artist, writer and photographer who lives in Arizona alongside a menagerie of critters. She has nine published how-to-draw books available internationally.

If you are a fan of horror stories and tales,
you'll want to follow Undertaker Books.
We're bringing you stories to take to your grave.